1

FULL OF WONDERMENT

a novel

Josh Greenfield

"On the other side, when a traveler and his *horse* are in heart and plight, when his purse is full and the day before him, he takes the road only where it is clean or convenient"

Jonathan Swift

I didn't return to Homer that summer. You hear in the news, every so often, about an oil spill off the coast of Alaska, and you wonder where all the oil went. Did it affect the salmon run? Did it wash up on the beaches? Are there still college kids camped out there eating scrambled eggs? But if they don't go to Homer, surely they go somewhere else, a town outside of Rio, a village on an island in the Aegean, a plaza on the coast of Spain. There is something about the age, the early twenties, that gives rise to the desire for travel, for a confirmation of the belief that there really is something more than forty years of nine to five and a solid retirement fund, for a confirmation of the belief that if you walk half way with an open hand and a smile, someone will come the rest of the way to meet you. These are beliefs that can't be tested in your own home town, even if your town is a great city. They can only be tested by those who have the guts to pick up their moorings and head out, even if they are not entirely sure where they will wind up.

That's what it's all about, isn't it? Making mistakes? How many mistakes can you make in front of a video game? You can fail to meet your previous high score. I guess you can spill Pepsi on the joy stick, or whatever they call the control panel, but the potentials for screwing up in a meaningful way are limited. I had headed off to the North Country with a plane ticket home, so I suppose my potential for screwing up was limited as well. And I did make it back. It might take away some of the suspense, but you might as well know. And it's a good thing too, because I was in no condition. I set off with many of the same aspirations as the other college kids making similar journeys, but I set off with something else as well, an obsessive compulsive gene. It is not an overstatement to say that while I was canning fish and climbing mountains, a kind of madness was setting in. It was the earliest stages of a terribly debilitating disease known as severe obsessive compulsive disorder.

On the island of Manhattan, a support system awaited, headed by my father, a brilliant and experienced man who was deeply committed to my welfare. But before I could get help, I would have to get there. I almost went off in the other direction entirely, which would have been a huge mistake. It is one thing for the young to seek adventure. It is something else for the mentally ill to wander too far from home. By the Grace of God, I returned, and by the Grace of God, I have prospered.

Here's what you need to know, right from the very start. I could not have been more cautious by nature. I was determined to do well in school, so determined that I stayed in the library every night until midnight, until they came through and turned out the lights. Then I'd go and study some more, in some empty class room in some deserted building. You'd think someone might have figured out that there was something wrong here, but for the time being, I was on my own. College life agreed with me in many ways. I shared a house with ten other students, boys and girls, who had decided to invest in the communal household. We ate dinner together five nights a week, all ten or eleven of us. Two people cooked and cleaned up, but I wanted out, this may have been a symptom of the illness which was to strike me years later, but I just wanted out.

I wanted out all the time, but now there were no more classes, no more exams, and I was gone, as good as gone, not to Trumansburg, not to New York City, not even to L.A. I was gone as far as I could possibly go and continue to speak the English language. The plan was vague; get on a plane, work in a cannery, make a lot of money, hit the road, hit it hard. Leave. That was the other part. Go as far away as possible. How I went, where I went were of secondary importance. Keep going. Keep going and never come back. Never? That was the question. This prestigious institution would be around four, five, ten years from now. The endowment was well managed, the libraries well maintained. Yes, the thought was there. Start traveling and keep going. There were no shortage of places to see, money to be made, mountains to be climbed, rivers to be forded. I know it sounds like some friggin' Oscar Hammerstein musical. What can I say? I was young. I was idealistic, and I had a couple of bucks for plane fare.

I'd had a life. I'd studied in the library. I'd eaten cream of broccoli soup. I attended class without fail, and when the stress of the whole thing became overwhelming, I fantasized about rolling down the hill and taking the next bus out of town. But all that time I'd wanted out I never did leave. I did what I was supposed to. I wrote the papers, took the mid-terms and accumulated the credits. I was in step with my classmates, and moving toward my degree. I had a major, an adviser and a projected graduation date. I knew the campus. I knew the routines, and there was nothing standing between me and a valuable Ivy League diploma. How quickly we decide to throw it all away! I never "dropped out." Even in the darker days to come, it was always a "leave of absence." I never turned my back on higher education. I simply considered the possibility of deferring the whole thing for a while. But when does a step off the track become a step too far? When does a train trip through a mountain pass become journey so far removed from the halls of academia that any idea of return becomes unacceptable? You can go out "on the road," but can you come back? The open sky may beckon, but if you fly too high your wings might melt. You might not make it home at all.

So I sat there on the ground floor of Olin Library, and turned the pages of one of the many atlases they kept on hand for the perusal of their graduate clientele. Cornell University is known for its libraries, and I'm not just saying that because they offered to put in a cot for me on the seventh level stacks. Architecturally, and in terms of their collections, they really are outstanding. The two main libraries stand across from each other on the central walkway leading from the Arts Quad to the central union. To the right is Uris Library, the undergraduate library, with its exquisite reading rooms and picture windows looking out over Cayuga Lake and valley below. On the left is Olin Library, a more functional structure with a world class research collection, designed for the research projects of graduate students and faculty. Both libraries were open to the public, an ID only being required to enter the Olin stacks, and it was on the ground floor of that graduate library where I sat to contemplate my future.

I had a destination in mind, the great state of Alaska. The state may not amount to much in the quadrennial role call to determine the next nominee of the Democratic Party for president of the United States, their contribution to the Electoral College still amounting to three votes, but it wasn't an exercise in politics that attracted me. I suppose it was, in a word, adventure. Alaska remained untamed, at least in my mind it did. The days of the Gold Rush had passed, but untrained workers were still working twelve hour shifts to the bitter cold and darkness of Trudeau Bay and making the kind of money office clerks and junior executives could only fantasize on their way from their office cubicle to the water cooler. In 1982, oil was being drilled, sled dogs were racing across the tundra, if not in earnest, at least in fun, and above all, and this was the catch, salmon were being canned during the summer.

The fact was incontrovertible. Every summer thousands of young people were being hired to process those fish, or can them, or freeze them, or do something with those damn fish. The issue here, it seemed to me, was getting yourself in the right place to take part, and it wasn't going to happen by sitting on the ground floor of a research library, however well stocked or carefully cataloged. Steps had to be taken. I closed the atlas and left it lying on the table. For a moment I looked out through the plate glass window at the arts quad, beginning to assume its summer colors. I got up and walked out of the library.

I'd gotten used to walking around alone. I had no insightful explanation for why this had happened. I'd just noticed the fact. We're talking about a major university, not some cliquish arts college. There were thousands and thousands of people. That in fact is, part of what had attracted me in the first place, a chance to go it alone, to find your own way. Still, I had noticed that I was moving around on my own. I wouldn't say it worried me. It was more of an observation. I turned to the left and joined in the flow of students moving toward Willard Straight Hall. I may have looked up. I may have looked down, but in my mind was the distinct idea that I was now going to go as far away as I possibly could. I never hated Cornell. There could be an overwhelming amount of pressure. There are jokes about the Ivy League that express an element of truth. "Cornell is the easiest one to get into, and hardest one to get out." I don't doubt it. But I never hated it. There was a girl, man was there a girl, and there were my housemates, and there was the work, which was in its own distorted way interesting. It was just that at this particular moment I had set my mind set on moving on, cutting out, splitting, getting aboard some mode of transportation and taking it to the end of the line. I was out of there.

Must have been about a two weeks later, ten days possibly, but there I was, slamming the door of my parents' maroon BMW, hoisting a worn, orange backpack on to one shoulder and activating the automatically opening doors of the TWA terminal at New York City's Kennedy Airport. I'd talked on the phone to a high school friend the night before, and told him I might go to the airport, puke and come home. The nausea levels were low. I had a reservation on a late morning flight to Seattle. I entered the terminal, set the pack on the ground, and took a seat on one of the metal benches that line the wall. I rested my head on the top of my pack and breathed deeply. I had my guitar. It was an old nylon string acoustic, what's called a classical guitar but I played it with a pick. I'd been strumming away for quite a few years, starting I guess with Joe Hill, and moving on through Pete Seeger and James Taylor. It's a wonderful calling card, the guitar, a great way to strike up a new acquaintanceship. It's also good company when you're traveling alone. The fantasy of the day was definitely Arlo Guthrie, not Woody, Arlo. And not the political Arlo of *Alice's Restaurant*, this was about the *Hobo's Lullaby*, *The Last Train to Glory*, walking down the highway, and letting the trains go slowly by. I had no plans to jump on any moving trains, but if the opportunity arose, I was fully prepared.

The first order of business was to get on a plane, and evidently, I made it to the departure gate on time. I was seated in the window seat, somewhere just behind the wing. I would have an unobstructed view of my transcontinental journey. The plane rumbled down the runway and took flight, banked to the left and ascended toward the low-lying clouds. The houses and streets of Queens assumed their undignified role of toy figures on a giant board game, and then disappeared from view entirely. For a moment, the plane was engulfed in the grey mist of clouds before we suddenly broke through to the blue and white wonderland above. How can you top that? What mountain landscape can hope to compare with the white spires and crystal blue sky of the world above the clouds, the shifting masses of clouds and the bright orange sunlight? Roll the credits,

strike up the music! I was on my way. I was bound for the north country, for

Alaska, for crying out loud. The doubts and the worries were left behind beneath

the overcast skies of New York. I had a backpack, a guitar, and what resembled a

destination. I sat back in my seat and let the waves of sheer excitement flow

through my body.

There is a sub-plot here, represented by a folded picture in my wallet. Her

name was Connie, and she had a face that was too beautiful for her own good, or

anyone else's for that matter. I'd seen her standing at a bus stop at the beginning

of fall semester, and that was it for me. What Connie had you couldn't buy for

love or money, the beauty that gets inside your head and gives you no peace, not

when you wake up in the morning, not when you go to sleep at night, not at any

time in between either. I had it, and I had it bad. It wasn't that I wanted to marry

the girl. I didn't hear wedding bells, and we were both so screwed up that we

could barely kiss. But I could think about her, and I did, most of the time.

Was my journey for Connie? Was I some kind of Arthurian Knight out to

prove his value to his lady? Certainly, that was part of it. I wrote her letters, I

called her on a borrowed credit card number, and when the trip was over I sat with

her on the roof of a boarding house in Berkeley, California. But have I ever forgiven her? A human being doing the best she could? No doubt. A huge component of my thought process, on my journey and before and after, but a person I parted ways with. Who am I to judge? Who am I to look into another person's soul? She was a beauty, of that there can be no doubt, and she stepped forth into this world with her own load to bear. For a time we were friends, groping make-out partners and better than that, we threw snow balls at each other in the corridor of the central campus class room building. She came to my aid when she thought I was ailing and cheered me on when I held on to a dream. And now it is past. But on that trip, that hair-brained journey to can fish in Alaska, she was my constant companion. I carried her picture, obtained from a mutual friend, in my wallet, and looked at it upon going to sleep and upon waking, upon laying down in a tent beside the side of a side road, when there was no ride to take me further, and while sitting on the car-seat that served as a couch beside the wooden shack that served as a home. I composed a song in her honor, and worked my way toward her in the Bay Area of California. If I'd paid more attention, I might remember how Don Quixote felt toward his woman, as he traveled across the land. Unfortunately, I can't recall. But maybe we had something in common.

Anyway, there I was jetting along above the clouds, on my way to Seattle. In Seattle I was to transfer to another flight that would take me to Anchorage,

Anchorage, AK. It doesn't take much to make this kind of trip in the twentieth century, a credit card to make a reservation, and the guts to fight down the nausea and walk through the airport. You walk through the front door of the airplane in New York City, and a few hours later you walk out the front door of another airplane in Alaska, no covered wagons, no sled dogs, not even a station wagon filled with screaming kids. You're just there with barely time to reflect on the distance you've traveled. I saw the countryside move by below me. When the clouds parted I saw the perfectly aligned squares of farmland in the mid-west, many with perfectly inscribed circles inside. I saw the huge chain of the Rocky Mountains rising up in distance and passing below, no more than a snow topped toy replica of the colossal achievement they represented. I ate my smoked almonds and the chicken dish they served for lunch. An elderly woman seated to my right talked to me about her son, his job and his prospects. She listened to my plans and may have understood more than she let on.

In Seattle, I transferred to another smaller plane for the next leg into the wild unknown. The flight was uneventful, but unfortunately, in the brief turnaround time in Seattle, my luggage did not make the connection. I arrived in the big city airport of Anchorage, Alaska without my backpack and guitar. This was a problem. Not a large problem, but a problem none the less. I spoke with the appropriate authorities, determined that my belongings would arrive the next day and boarded the city bus bound for the Anchorage Youth Hostel, a stranger in a strange town, or should I say an innocent abroad. I don't know the origin of either phrase, but I would say the later was somewhat more appropriate. Each city, I believe, has its own manner of riding public transportation, a manner developed over generations, and passed on from one to the next. New York City's may be one of the most incomprehensible to outsiders. When a New Yorker rides the subway, he knows just what he is doing, and the manner of a new comer is evident to all. It is for this reason, perhaps, that most tourists confine themselves to a five-block radius surrounding Times Square, and the upper deck of a tour bus. But New York is not alone. Anchorage too has its habits and customs. I may not have been the first these locals had witnessed, but I was clearly a summer worker from the lower forty-eight, or at the very least, a stranger who had no idea where to look or how to conduct himself. They smiled, they may have chuckled. Even without the orange backpack I stood out.

Youth hostels around the globe share certain things in common, things beyond an area for preparing food and sleeping room with multiple beds. They are the resting place for the person on the go, usually a young person, but not always, an oasis if you will, in which to let down your guard, if only a little, and breath deeply in a place far from home. The first night in the Anchorage Youth Hostel was spent in the company of prospective gold prospectors. I kid you not. I was assigned to a bunk in a large room on the first floor where the predominant conversation concerned means of distilling gold dust from sand, and shooting bears. Were these guys serious? This was well into the second half of the twentieth-century. Someone was missing something here, and I don't think it was me. I lay on my bunk and refrained from contributing to the discussion. I was on the lookout for useful information, but it did not concern panning for gold or mining gold or doing anything else with gold. As far as I was concerned, gold had dropped out of the picture somewhere in the last century. What I needed was information on canning salmon. Now there was something practical. A city kid who spent his time in a library in western New York was going to make big money in the salmon business. That was reality.

My luggage arrived. Alaskan Airlines came through. The next morning both my orange backpack and my guitar were waiting for me at the service desk of the Anchorage City Airport. I returned to the youth hostel, even more conspicuous than the day before encumbered my two badges of honor that clearly indicated I was not from the neighborhood. That night I was moved to a room the second floor where my introduction to the cannery worker community began. How many of us were there? Certainly hundreds, probably thousands, young men and women who had traveled from literally every corner of the earth for the chance to make big money in a short amount of time. Some came to earn their next year's tuition, some to finance a pet project or dream. Many were travelers of the road for years at a time, who came through southern Alaska in the summer to finance the next leg of their journey. The California state colleges and universities were particularly well represented, but so were the Australians and the Israelis and college students from all across the country. We were all there to work hard and make money, but certainly we had more in common. We all had our heads in the clouds, or had had our heads in the clouds at some time along the way. We had all wanted out. And we had all gotten on a plane, or a boat or a long distance bus to make it happen.

The second floor of the Anchorage Youth Hostel is where I first met three young women, a older sister who had been there the year before and her two younger sisters who had been persuaded to come along this time. Before the summer was over, one of the younger sisters had met the man she would spend her life with, and for this, I was at least partially responsible. But on that first night, on the second floor the Anchorage Youth Hostel, none of us knew anything about this. I had found a real live cannery worker, someone who had had a successful summer in this business and was back for more. Here was someone who knew a thing or two. I wanted to know what she knew.

I had not arrived in Alaska completely ignorant. I'd spoken to people in Ithaca, and learned all I could. I'd heard of a town called Homer, Homer Alaska. To this day it arouses mythic associations in my mind. I tried to get there, got side tracked and later made the trip for a weekend outing. It was everything it was built up to be. Homer Alaska has the distinction of being at the southern tip of the Kenia Peninsula. It is situated on the end of spit of land and surrounded on three sides by water. Beyond the water, also on all three sides, are the kind of magnificent mountains that Alaskans take for granted, but that the rest of world finds suitable for a National Geographic Special. The town itself, unlike the rest of the Kenia Peninsula, would fit in nicely on the southern shore of Cape Cod, boasting art galleries and cafés. But at least during the summer, the big business in Homer is fish, salmon of every kind that must be processed and frozen and sent off to the lower forty-eight. And it is to perform this work that the young people come from far and wide. They work twelve-hour shifts, making time and a half after eight hours and during their off-time, they sleep on the beach looking out at those magnificent peaks. Thousands of young people, making lots of money and sleeping on the beach, they may have played in the mud at Woodstock, but for my money, nothing could top this.

I'd heard about Homer over the kitchen table in the Dryden Diner. A friend of a housemate had actually been there. Or so I'd heard. I'd gotten the broad outlines and from the very start, Homer had been my tentative destination. Here, on the second floor of the Anchorage Youth Hostel was a young woman who had done it, who had spent a summer there and was back for more. Yes, she had made a shit load of money. Yes, they slept on the beach. It all sounded good. We talked and it all sounded like fun, but I wasn't completely sold. I was open to other possibilities. There were at least two, tenders, and backcountry sites, not to mention other canneries on the Kenia Peninsula. Tenders were the most isolated, huge boats that moored somewhere off-shore and processed the salmon entirely on board. There was work here. The principle drawback was the difficulty in leaving. You gave away some of your freedom, and if you wanted to leave early, they could charge you. Backcountry sites had some of the same liabilities. The owner took on the expense of flying his workers to some remote location in western Alaska, or out on the Aleutian Islands. He paid them well for their labor. Here again, however, it seemed to me, it might be hard to leave. You were placing yourself very much in someone else's hands.

Nothing was resolved, but I'd made some acquaintances, and when I did finally make it down to Homer, with its famous beaches, I spent an evening with the three of them. The middle sister was not enamored with her situation and came back to work at A.O.P., which is where she met Darl, whom she later married. Hey, if the internet sites aren't working out, why not come on up to Kenia, eligible men, hardworking and adventurous. It worked out for them, as I happen to know, having seen them many years down the line. But as I said before, that first night, we didn't know anything about this. All was expectation, the beginning of a new season. I had the timing right. That I'd made sure of. The season for catching and processing salmon is tightly controlled by the fish and game authorities, and I'd made sure to arrive with plenty of time to hit it right.

The season was fast approaching, but it wasn't there yet. I had some time to explore my options, and the most logical place, it turned out, was the job service center in downtown Anchorage. The word was that a lot of people were getting hired out of here. Maybe it wasn't necessary to hitch down the peninsula. Maybe it could get work right there in Anchorage. Not to work in Anchorage, but to get hired by an employer recruiting in Anchorage. That was the possibility. And I was not alone. There they were the other cannery workers who had come from far and wide seeking adventure and big money in jobs the locals would only look on as a last resort. The job service center was a large institutional room in a large institutional building somewhere in downtown Anchorage. Anchorage didn't have a downtown the way New York has a downtown. There was no congregation of high rise building. It's a more spread out affair with a web of interlocking four lane roads. And somewhere in this spread of roads was the Anchorage job service center. An office established by the city of Anchorage for the benefit of both perspective employers and perspective employees. The idea here was to bring them together. It didn't work for me, but that is where I landed.

I spoke with one of the administrators and chatted with some of the other suckers on the lookout for work. It was here that my picture of the Alaskan summer salmon industry really filled out. I got a better picture of its various components, the tenders for those who worked liked being stationed at sea, and the backcountry sites for those who relished being far removed from CNN. There were the canneries on the Kenia Peninsula which could be reached via the hitch-hikers thumb and there was one final component, the fishing boats themselves. Work could be found on those boats by showing up at the docks and asking for it. This was potentially the most lucrative component of the whole system, and also potentially the most dangerous. There was an element of danger here. Knives were used in cleaning the fish and heavy machinery was employed to move things around. One co-worker was sent home with a badly maimed leg after getting it caught in an ice machine. But, in all honesty, these things did not concern me at the time. I was just trying to figure out what was going on, and trying to make the best decision.

What stands out in memory is not so much what happened in the job service center as what happened afterward. My breakdown was some two years in the future. I was a relatively normal guy, but the seeds were there, somewhere in my mind, beginning to take root, beginning to grow. At the heart of the matter was the anger. I knew nothing about it at the time and it took a brilliant psychiatrist years to drive it into my head, but I had a problem with anger, kind of like an allergy. Anger did not agree with me. It still doesn't, and it never will. There were plenty of other problems, but the anger thing was right at the bottom of it all. That evening, upon leaving the job service center I went out for a drink with two young guys I had met, who like myself were looking for work in the cannery business. They seemed nice enough, and we certainly had plenty to talk about. They had heard about a topless place that sold four dollar pitchers of beer, and that is where we went.

As topless bars go, this one was on the seedier side of the spectrum. They did have four dollar pitchers, and the three of us took a table and took in the scenery. We talked shop. They didn't have the whole thing figured out either, but they too were set on finding work. It was a congenial enough gathering. There was no great tension between the three of us. They may have known each other a bit, but it really wasn't an issue. Then trouble hit. One of the waitresses did what waitresses do in topless bars, she came over to give one of my drinking partners a lap dance. I did not remain for its conclusion. In barely an instant, I was through the front door of the bar and out on the sidewalk. With all the strength in my body, I lifted my green day pack in the air and smashed it down on the sidewalk. I didn't scream, but there was a loud thwack, as the backpack hit the concrete. I was alone. No one had noticed my action. I kneeled down and opened the pack to survey the damage.

It was a real *Easy Rider* moment. My traveling alarm clock, in its red folding vinyl case was broken. There was a crack across the face of the clock. I picked it up. It made no sound. Nothing was moving here. I closed the pack and began to walk slowly away. Some people can get angry, "the dubious luxury of normal men." I am not among them. Even a minor outbreak or "brainstorm" sends dangerous chemicals through my brain. The violent outburst takes it to an entirely different level. I was stoned. More accurately, I was tripping. The chemicals released by a violent anger are in fact identical to the chemicals released on an acid trip. So there I was, wandering through downtown Anchorage, wasted, high, disoriented and generally lost. I was living a Doors concert while people around me were returning home from work. I knew I had to get back to the youth hostel, but I was not at all sure how that was going to happen.

I walked left. I walked right. I knew I would have to take a bus, but I really didn't know where to begin to find the right bus stop. I asked directions. This time I didn't get chuckles, or even smiles, I got distracted stares, and backhanded gestures. I made my way to a bus stop and boarded a bus, and by nothing more than good fortune was brought to the vicinity of the youth hostel. I walked the last few blocks on foot, and as I walked my head began to clear. Little by little, the fog lifted. I began to see my surroundings with greater clarity, the sounds around me began to come in with less of a filter. This too is anger. Anger is not only a screaming match between a man and woman over an over extended budget. Anger is a chemical reaction that can last for hours and distort all perception. The skill here is not only refraining from the angry outburst in the first place, but also learning to decrease the time it lasts, skills not easily mastered.

I walked back into the youth hostel, found my way to my dorm room, and lay down on my bed. I took stock. It was time to move on. The big city was not agreeing with me. I had not come to Alaska to spend time in a city. I knew all about cities. I remained profoundly skeptical about the opportunities for employment available here. Back country sites, tenders, these things were not for me. What if I didn't like it? I'd never worked in a cannery before. What if the

whole thing didn't agree with me, and I wanted out? Those employers could make

things difficult. This too was not for me. I needed a cannery with a road by it, a

road traveled by every day ordinary cars, where a guy could hitch a ride, if he had

a mind to. That meant the Kenia Peninsula. It was quite clear. Where exactly on

the Kenia Peninsula I wasn't sure. There was Homer, but Homer had a draw back,

no bathrooms, no cabins. Sleeping on the beach sounded great and all, but I still

wondered about spending that much time outdoors. There were other possibilities.

I dropped off to sleep.

The new day found me even more resolved. It was time to move on. I

packed my bags, ate a quick breakfast, and prepared to hit the road. Isn't this what

it was all about? A backpack, a guitar and your thumb as a means of transportation?

There were no buses going where I wanted to go, or if there were, they went once

every third week. There was only one way to make this trip, the way generations

of hobos and tramps had done it before me. Hopping a train would also have been

suitable, but there were no trains going there either. I had a rough idea of the map

in my head. The Kenia Peninsula extends some hundred and fifty miles south

west of Anchorage. The town of Homer is way down on the end, but there were

other towns along the way, Soldatna to the east, and the town of Kenia itself on the western shore. That is where I was bound. If I made it as far as Homer, so be it, but if I got side tracked, that was O.K. too. Actually, I was on the lookout for a cannery down there that had cabins and showers. I'd pass up some of the spectacular scenery for an enclosed bathroom and a bed with a roof over it.

Everyone knows you can't start a hitch-hiking trip in the middle of a city. Even I knew that, and I was a relative new comer to the whole business. There were highways that headed south west but to get on one, I would have to get out of town. This time I knew which bus to take, and in the early morning hours, of a Saturday morning, I stood and waited for the bus to arrive. My pack rested against my right led, and my black cardboard guitar case lay on the ground to my right. I wore blue jeans and a white T-shirt with a picture of a kayak negotiating a white water rapid. I was traveling alone. Before leaving New York I had attempted to persuade a couple of old friends to make the trip. One had a chance to learn carpentry skills, another was learning Russian in preparation for a trip abroad and a third just didn't have the heart for it. So there I was quite alone, alone in a way people just aren't since the invention of the cell phone. The sky was blue. The sun was shining, and I was off to look for work.

As I waited for my bus to arrive I withdrew my maroon canvas wallet from my back pocket, and released the Velcro closure. Inside, covered in clear plastic, was Connie's picture. She was laughing. She wore her brown, waist length, down jacket, open at the neck, and she was looking into the camera and laughing. The very thought that someone would want to take her picture was so ridiculous that it made her laugh, but in her own way she was a friend to the camera, long auburn hair reflecting the sunlight, deep green eyes and a quizzical smile that rejected categorization. She had turned down her mother's advice to become a pediatrician and instead enrolled in the engineering school, the most rigorous curriculum at Cornell, a school known for its rigorous curriculums. That past spring she'd taken twenty-three credits, which is a few steps beyond ridiculous. She knew how gorgeous she was, there was no way she could have avoided that fact, but for the most part she chose to disregard it.

I quietly refastened the Velcro strip and replaced the wallet in my pocket. I would write another letter as soon as things settled down. An Anchorage city bus turned the corner down the block and approached the stop. "An Anchorage city bus," even the name of it had romance. This was no Broadway local, or Seventy-Ninth Street cross town. This was Anchorage, Alaska, the major city in the fiftieth state, the last frontier, the land of the mid-night sun. Maybe Hawaii came in after Alaska, but who really cared. Did Hawaii have an Anchorage city bus? I think not. I lifted my pack and picked up my guitar and boarded. Early Saturday morning, a few travelers headed out to the suburbs, if that's what they are called in Anchorage. I stutter stepped my way to the rear of the bus, my orange pack bumping against my right thigh as I moved. I took a seat on the right side and tried to look non-shall-ant. Sure doesn't everyone travel around with a pack and a guitar? What's the big deal here?

But I wasn't the only one on that bus with a guitar. Across the aisle, a couple of seats to the, rear was a young guy holding a steel string acoustic. He had no case. Just the guitar lying loosely across his lap, and he was playing it. The engines kicked in, the breaks released, the bus started down the road. I tried not to stare, but my musical traveling partner clearly was not self-conscious. He made eye contact and kept on playing.

"Ventura Highway, in the sunshine,

Where the days are longer and the nights are stronger than moonshine.

I want to go, I know.

'Cause the free wind is blowing thought your hair

and the day light shining everywhere.

I want to go."

I knew the song. A hit by the band America, probably didn't sell as many copies as *Horse with No Name*, but a minor classic in its own right. So now top this, I'm on an Anchorage city bus being driven to the open highway, and this guy is

singing me an America song. There was no way.

I listened. The bus made its way through suburban Anchorage, quiet tree

lined streets of one family houses. The day was new. The musician finished his

song and proceeded to play chords and riffs. I watched him play. At one stop,

seemingly very little different than the one before, he got up, holding his guitar in

his right arm, and exited the rear of the bus. He didn't look at me. Well that was

it. Now I was really on my own. My instructions had been to take the number

eighteen bus to the end of the line, and that is just what I was going to do. When

the bus stopped moving, and didn't start up again, I would get off. I turned toward

the front of the bus and watched the world go by. We may have been moving

through the suburbs of a major city, but there were indications that this was not

Phoenix or New Orleans. Off in the distance, visible through the breaks in the

trees, were a range of mountains the like of which I'd never seen before. Huge,

awesome affairs in shades of blue and grey, topped with massive patches of white

snow. I'd seen them descending into the airport, but now I was going to encounter

them on a first-hand basis.

The bus pulled to a stop, and the driver applied the hand break. I hoisted

my back pack this time slipping both arms through the arm straps and walked to the front of the bus to exit properly my guitar in hand. The driver made no remark.

We were a sign of the season, college age kids who came into the state from the

lower forty-eight, with backpacks and guitars. Their everyday lives had become a

destination and maybe it conferred a degree of pride. I turned sideways and edged

down the three steps to street level. There was no one about. No private houses.

No tree lined streets. The bus had come to rest along the margins of a two-lane

highway that sloped away to the right. It had taken me exactly where I needed to

be, to the exact point where I might begin the next leg of my journey, this time

traveling through the courtesy of strangers. I took a few steps down the road and

looked back over my shoulder at the bus driver. He had already taken out the

morning paper.

I kept walking. I was looking for a straight section of road. I could feel my

heart beating in my chest.

"Now you've really gone and done it," I thought. "Now you've really gone

and done it."

And there they were, those damn mountains, up close and in person.

"Awesome" was a popular word in 1982. Some T.V. star on some sit-com had

started using it, and it was going around to the extent that it had lost all meaning.

Here the word applied. The mountains off to my right, standing beyond an inlet of icy grey water were awesome. I set my pack down on the ground, opened the rear flap and removed a bag of granola cereal and a bag of prunes. I sat on the pack and had a snack. The occasional car drove by. The car of choice up here seemed to be a pick-up with a shot gun mounted in the rear-view mirror. I attracted very little attention, but I took in the view and breathed the clear morning air. It was still sunny, but some large white clouds had started to float in from the south, or the west or where ever they were floating in from, huge billowy affairs that matched the shapes of the mountains they surrounded. There was a large body of water just down the embankment to the right of the roadway. The mountain range began on the far side. This was an extension of the Cook Inlet, a tidal basin with incredibly dramatic shifts between high and low tide. The water rushes in and rushes out, twice a day, again on the order of a phenomenon worthy of National Geographic.

But all of this was back drop. I had serious business at hand. I polished off one more prune, replaced the bag, along with the granola, in my pack and prepared to get down to business. Some hitch hikers will swear by the utility of a sign, and under certain circumstances, I concur, it can be useful. If the potential ride is coming to a fork in the road, he may want to know which way you intend to go. Why would he want to pick you up if he can only take you a couple of miles? A sign can also show a certain seriousness of purpose. It can show that the hitch hiker has thought things through and does in fact have a destination in mind. But in this occasion I did not have a sign. Partially because the road I was on only led in one direction, and partially because I didn't know exactly where I was going. I did have a backpack and guitar, which were effective signs that I was a legitimate traveler and not someone who had been sleeping it off in the back room of a bar and missed his ride. The guitar was featured front and center. Next to hitch hiking with a woman, a guitar is among the best signs that a single male hitch hiker means no harm. I stuck out my thumb.

I had chosen to stand toward the far end of a straight length or road. This gives the approaching car time to look you over before they make the big decision. It also gives them space to pull over without causing a traffic hazard. I may never have hitch hiked down the Kenia Peninsula before, but I'd done it enough to know this. So I waited. That too is a big part of hitch hiking, waiting. It is not the preferred mode of transportation for those in a hurry. To be content as a hitch hiker you really want to have no time tables at all.

"It's about the journey, man," completely true.

You may have some place you would like to arrive, eventually, but if you're in a big rush to get there, it isn't going to be much fun. Humor can be another part of it. Some hitch hikers prefer to remain dignified, no doubt, but I always felt that if

you could get a smile out of the approaching driver, you'd have a better chance of

getting a ride. Break them up, or try, just a little. Put the thumb behind your back,

something. This can also help relieve the monotony.

So there I stood, orange Kelty pack positioned strategically against my front

leg, black guitar case clearly visible to my right, the picture of youth and idealism,

a figure to make Arlo or even Woody proud. I stood proudly as a representative of

the lower forty-eight come to fill a seasonal labor shortage on the last frontier, and

all I needed was some someone to give me a ride to work. And surprise, surprise,

someone stopped. I use the generic carefully, "someone" stopped. It was a

scarred and tattered blue VW van with no side door, no side door at all. The front

wind shield had a crack in it. The paint was rubbed off, repainted and rubbed off

again. This van was not well. But hell, it was a ride. Someone had actually

stopped to pick me up. I quickly pulled on my pack, picked up my guitar and

scampered down the road to the point where my unfortunate van had pulled to a

stop.

At this point you might think that the better part of judgment might kick in.

Nowhere is it written that the hitch hiker must take every ride that is offered.

There are polite or flat out blunt ways of conveying the fact that you have no interest in getting in the friggin' car, no way, no how, not if your life depended on it. I did not chose to convey this fact. I opened the passenger side door,

"Thanks a lot," I panted, still slightly out of breath from my jog down the road.

"Throw it in back," the driver looked at my pack and motioned with his head to the back of the van.

Here again, the better part of judgment might have kicked in. The driver was a man in his early sixties with a grey, unkempt beard. He wore blue jeans and old cracked work boots. His shirt was also of denim, fastened with snaps but open almost to the waist. But the appearance of the driver was not the disturbing part of this picture, or not the only part. Lying on the front seat of the van, practically in open view, with only a plaid work shirt thrown casually over them, were three or four clear, empty whiskey bottles. I kid you not. The first ride offered to me on my journey south was from a bona-fide alcoholic, a guy who appeared to be braced for the long haul.

But what did I know from alcoholism? My encounter with the Big Book lay years in the future. So the guy had a few bottles in his car. Maybe he was into arts and crafts. Maybe he enjoyed making candle holders. It really didn't concern me. Or should I say, I chose not to let it concern me. I stepped back and carefully stowed the pack and guitar in the rear of the van, in a position from which they would not be likely to fly out on a strong left turn. I climbed into the passenger seat.

"You got a license?" the white-haired gentleman asked me.

This was his opening gambit. Not "Where you bound?" or "Beautiful day." but "You got a license?"

There was still time. I could have climbed out of that van, left the door open to prevent him from driving off while I removed my stuff, and walked away. In general terms however, I was a pretty polite fellow, and this didn't seem neighborly. I looked out the front window, as the decrepit, blue van, with no side door pulled away from the curb. There are standard variants of conversation common shortly after a hitch hiker takes a ride. Among the first order of business is,

"Where are you going?"

Also covered, early on is,

"Where are you from?" and,

"How's the hitch hiking been going in these parts?"

If the driver did some hitch hiking in his own day, he might like to share some of his own war stories. Nobody forces these people to stop. They do it out of their own free will and the desire to help another human being who needs a lift, physically, and possibly emotionally, considering that he may have been standing by the side of the road for some prolonged period of time. Generally, the interaction is sociable. The driver might be lonely and want to talk, out west it could be a Mormon who sees the chance to proselytize. My first ride down the Kenia Peninsula was from a guy who had another agenda. He was a drunk, driving without a license. In my youth, my innocence or my enthusiasm, or some combination of the three, however, this fact went right by me.

He seemed to be holding the road pretty well, and it was not such an easy road to hold. Just two lanes, one headed north and one headed south, with the south bound land abutting what amounted to a steep precipice. The top of the precipice was protected by a fence of two inches, thick wire cable, two rows supported periodically by metal stanchions. Dropping off precipitously on the far side of the fencing, was a dirt slope leading down to a body of frigid water, the Cook Inlet, which may or may not have been at high tide. Beyond the water, rising magnificently from the far coast line were a range of mountains I could not have named, but which were certainly worthy of attention, if not a photograph or two. Since stepping into the van, however, I had my mind on other things.

He wasn't talking. He was driving, and I had my first ride. Now I was really going places, where I wasn't exactly sure, but I was certainly moving. There was the issue of the whiskey bottles. There they were, clanking around on the front seat beside me, their sound only partially muffled by the plaid shirt. But I didn't go into it just then.

"How far are you going," that's what I wanted to ask, to get some idea of how far he was planning on driving, but as I said, he wasn't exactly welcoming conversation.

"You travel with a license?" There was that question again. I had managed to avoid it the first time around.

"Yes. I do. New York State…," I didn't completely follow his line of reasoning, and he didn't say anything more.

"How far are you traveling, this morning," I ventured, the door having been opened.

"A ways down, past Clam Gulch…, "and that was it. I actually didn't have any idea where Clam Gulch was, and "a ways down" was thoroughly ambiguous. The driver made no attempt to ascertain where I would like to be left off. He had a driver with a license in the van. I guess that was good enough for him

So I looked at the scenery. Both the driver side and the passenger side windows were open, not to mention the ventilation coming in through the missing door out back. It was not easy to converse any way, what with all that wind blowing. We bounced along, high up off the road way and I looked at the mountains, the water and the mountains, a striking combination, set beside each other like that. The clouds were still coming in, and it wasn't the same clear morning it had been at the bus stop in Anchorage, but there were still patches of blue above. I thought about Connie. She'd chosen a more stable line of work. She was a waitress at a café in her home town of Berkeley, California, her brother's café, Expresso Roma. I couldn't take out her picture, under the circumstances, but I visualized it, that brown down jacket, strategically cut to the waist, and her hair, of which she was justifiably proud. The hair went below the waist and it was thick and auburn, not red, auburn, and treated with care. Hadn't she dressed up as the woman in the Clairol advertisement that Halloween night, that one night.

Wake up man…Earth to Jordan….There's a car ride going on here… a van ride…keep your wits about you….please. But nothing had changed. The driver was staring straight ahead, his right hand poised casually on the apex of the steering wheel, his left hand on his left thigh. His gaze was languid, possibly thoughtful, or maybe just empty. He kept his eyes on the road, but he wasn't paying all that much attention. I looked back at the scenery. Clam Gulch… I tried to place it on the map, but came up empty, must have been one of those small towns along the coast but I had no idea how far down. Well, if this ride ended, there could always be another. He'd stopped quickly. I'd hardly had my thumb out five minutes.

"You looking for work?" The driver kept looking straight ahead, but spoke to me.

"Uh-huh," I answered.

"Plenty of work once the salmon start running," there was very little variation in the tone of his voice, but he was holding the road just fine.

"That's what I'm counting on," I kept things going.

He went back to driving, and I looked out the window. What the hell did I really know any way? Some people called them canneries, some people called them cold storage. Either you cooked the fish and put them in cans, or you froze them whole, that seemed to be the distinction. I'd never done either. And twelve hour shifts. Who ever heard of working twelve hours in a row? Another crazy idea. I turned to my traveling partner.

"What do you know about it? About cannery work?

He didn't seem to hear me, just kept driving, his right hand resting casually on top of the steering wheel, his eyes fixed on the road ahead. His eyes weren't half closed, but the eye balls seemed to have floated suspiciously close to the top of eye sockets. I wasn't sure how much he was taking in. Add to that the fact that the wind was still blowing from every direction and the prospects for conversation seemed slim.

"Clean work," He finally volunteered. "Everybody thinks a cannery smells of fish. It ain't so. The fish come in and gets frozen the same day. There ain't no smell. Not if the plant's run properly. It's the old fish that starts to smell. If a plant is processing old fish it's a poorly run plant," That was it. He shut down and went back to driving.

Well I'd learned something new. A plant that processes old fish is a poorly run plant. I'd have to watch out for that, if I ever got inside a plant to find out. Maybe it would be Homer after all. Homer had the mystery. Homer had the magic, and if I kept on going south, I'd wind up there. We'd been on the road for some forty-five minutes at this point, and were traveling inland, away from the water, but the mountains were still clearly visible in the distance. It had turned into a warm, hazy summer's day. Beneath my feet on the floor of the van were the remnants of someone's lunch, nothing alive here, just some Styrofoam packaging and a colored paper bag. Resting on the dashboard, at the far right hand end, and being blown around by the wind, was a crumpled Budweiser can. I didn't bother to turn and look in the back, it didn't seem polite, but my pack and guitar were still secure. I had tucked them behind a piece of machinery that resembled a leaf blower. It was covered with dust, however, and didn't look like it would be blowing leaves, or anything else, any time soon. The back of the van also held other rakes, shovels, and implements of destruction. Their presence on the metal floor added to the general commotion of the moment, but like the leaf blower they did not seem to be eager of service. I tried again.

"How far down is Clam Gulch?" I tried to sound casual.

"Just outside of Kenia," he saw fit to respond.

Well that added to the picture. I'd heard tell of a cannery in Kenia that was supposed to furnish its employees with cabins, cabins and a bathroom. Playing in the mud at Woodstock for three days must have been grand, but we were talking about six weeks here, six weeks of hard work, and I had to admit, these amenities sounded attractive. It was nothing definite. A rumor, more or less, picked up at the hostel, or the job service center. The place had a name, Alaska Ocean Products, and it was down there somewhere, somewhere near the town of Kenia. I concentrated on my view out the passenger side window. No point in letting the place go by unannounced.

We kept on. All told we were driving for a couple of hours, without much conversation to show for it when, up ahead on the right, a small restaurant came into a view. I'm tempted to call it a coffee shop, but that's kind of an Upper West-Side thing. They don't have coffee shops in Alaska. They have roadside restaurants, and that is where the driver was taking us. He pulled into the lot, and stopped the van with a lurch. He climbed out, making no attempt to ascertain whether I was interested in a tuna sandwich, or a BLT on rye, or whatever they ate up here. I got out and followed him in.

It was a simple joint with a sparkling view of the road. It had a wooden counter, four square tables, arranged with no great care for symmetry, and a juke box that was not playing. There was one woman standing behind the counter, who was not particularly interested in the fact that she had two new potential customers, which was two more than the zero she had before. She was young enough to be attractive, but old enough to have hair streaked in grey. She also really didn't seem to care. Her hair was pulled back in a loose pony tail and she wore a print blouse, in shades of blue buttoned up close to her chin. There was a hint of a smile on her face when my companion came in and she reached under the counter for an empty coffee cup. She walked down to the end of the bar, or counter, or whatever you call it and poured a hot black cup of Jo. There was a slight wisp of steam coming from the cup as she placed it before him along with a small metal pitcher of milk. Don't ask me how I remember all this. I guess some things, some scenes, just stay with you. Don't know why that is.

"How's it going, Brad?" the counter attendant asked quietly.

I'm not a big coffee drinker, and there seemed to be some kind of connection going on here, so I wandered down to look at the juke box. It was unplugged, or broken. The window showed a flip page of Jimmy Buffet and The Four Tops. An odd combination, I thought, but I couldn't listen to anything anyway, so it was no big deal. I sat down at one of the tables and thought about Connie. It didn't look like we were going anywhere. Not right away, anyway. I was aware that this whole experience was violating the norms of hitch-hiking. Here I was sitting in some roadside rest stop waiting for my ride to drink coffee. Granted, he could probably use some coffee, but I couldn't help thinking I'd be better off out on the road, actually going someplace.

I looked around the simple restaurant. Evidently, they served beer, there was a large display advertising Rolling Rock Beer on the far, right hand wall. Funny, my guy had gone for the coffee. Just as well. Our mode of transportation was none too stable to begin with. It could use a driver fully unimpaired. The four tables were each covered with a red check table cloth, and each featured a metal container of sugar, no sweet and low, just sugar. My table had a salt shaker, the one to my right had pepper. The other two had neither. The waitress called over

from behind the counter.

"Coffee?"

"No. No thanks," I replied.

I turned and looked out the front door, and waited for Brad, if that was his

name, to finish up. But it was still about Connie, she'd have to hear about this one,

Brad, the van, Jimmy Buffet…couldn't say how seriously she took the letters

really, but she'd hear about it all anyway. Brad was through. He and the waitress

had been talking quietly. I didn't know he had it in him, that much conversation,

but I didn't really want to know what they were talking about. He pulled a

crumpled dollar bill out of his jeans pocket and left in on the counter. We walked

outside.

Brad started the engine, which responded with a growl and a roar and we

pulled out of the parking area.

"I'll be heading over to Soldatna up a ways," he didn't look at me.

Well, here we go, I thought. This ride is through.

"Would that be on the far side of Kenia?" I asked.

"Uh-huh," He seemed to have used up all his conversation with the waitress.

"Then I'll be getting off on the far side of town." Is that what they called it,

"The far side of town?"

And that is just what I did. We passed through the roaring metropolis of Kenia, AK, with its three stop lights, a laundromat, a liquor store, and two bars, and back on to the road that had served us so well. We approached an intersection with an option to turn off to the east. The driver, Brad to those who knew him well, pulled the decrepit blue van, with its rakes and shovels and implements of destruction rattling around in the back, over to the side of the road. I opened the door to get out. There still wasn't a whole lot to say.

"Thanks for the ride," I said.

Brad didn't look at me.

"You got it," he said.

I took a few steps toward the rear of the van and carefully removed my pack and guitar from behind the leaf blower. Brad reared around to the left and drove off.

There may be romance in the Anchorage city bus, but it was nothing compared with this. The day was getting on and I was standing by the side of some road, somewhere on the Kenia Peninsula. There was a thick growth of tall grass at my feet, and at my back were those magnificent mountains, huge and awe inspiring. I'd been alone before, but nothing like has. For the time being you might say that I'd "really gone and done it." There was no traffic. I was starting to consider the possibility that I might be stranded here for the night. I traveled with a tent and a sleeping bag tied to the top and bottom of my pack respectively, and I was prepared to down right there if it came to that. The occasional pick-up straggled down the road and I stuck out my thumb, but they showed very little interest. I reached in my pack for a snack, and sat there eating dry granola and prunes. I was content. This is exactly what I had signed up for. I'd gone just about as far as you can go, and continue to speak the English language. Only on this occasion I had no one to speak it with. I could sleep there. That would be fine.

I pulled on my pack, and started walking down the road, the hitch-hiker's illusion that he is actually making progress,

"At least I'm walking," the thought goes.

And then it happened. Don't mean to be overly dramatic, but "it happened." Up ahead on the right-hand side of the road was a large rectangular sign, and as I approached, I made out the words, "Alaska Ocean Products," in black letters on a green background, no graphics.

"Well, what the heck?" I said quietly to myself.

As I approached the sign it became apparent that there was some kind of dirt driveway leading off the road to the right.

"Evidently," I thought, "This is the place."

I reached the top of a small hill, trudging along with my orange backpack, and guitar in hand, and took the right-hand turn. I was excited, certainly. Here seemingly out of dumb luck, I had stumbled on the very place I had in mind at the outset. A cannery, or cold storage operation, accessible by road, that was rumored to provide cabins and indoor plumbing. Only a moment before I had considered myself to be on the very edge of civilization and here I was walking into the Promised Land.

I made my way down the dirt drive way. The soil was an orangeish brown, and the underbrush was thick on either side. I knew I was walking toward the water, the Cook Inlet, which had been to my right the whole way down. As I descended the dirt roadway I began to hear a peculiar sound. It sounded like young people playing a game, laughing and calling to one another. And that is just what it was. I rounded a curve at the foot of the drive way that opened on to a large parking lot, a lot with no cars in it. To the left, was a huge metal shed, a couple of hundred feet long, with open doorways leading into a darkened interior. Not much was happening in there. On the far side of the lot were rows of wooden box like structures. They were constructed of simple unfinished plywood with a door cut in one side, and a square for a window on the opposing wall. Straight ahead, between these functional structures was the waterfront with the mountains beyond. The water itself was screened by a growth of brush and small trees. It was getting on toward evening, and one of the endless Alaskan summer sunsets was beginning its brilliant dance across the sky.

I took all this in, at a glance, but what really attracted my attention was the activity within the lot itself. Five young people were throwing a Frisbee. They appeared to be blissfully uninformed that we were somewhere on the edge of civilization, and that people were striving for employment. They were playing catch. So I dropped my bags, and went to join them. It seemed the only sociable thing to do. In less than a half an hour I had made the transition from frontier explorer, alone in the West, to college sophomore on a college campus in some New England college town, or prep school. There was nothing foreign here. There was nothing alien. Just a bunch of kids, kind of like me, and that in fact is what they turned out to be. Two kids out from Oberlin, one of whom played on the Oberlin Ultimate Frisbee Team, a sport coming into vogue in the early eighties, one a recent graduate from Northfield Mount Herman, a prep school, my prep school played in football, two high school seniors up from California, just a couple of years younger than myself. Just when you think you've gone where no man has gone before, you realize a whole bunch other people had the same idea, and got there first.

So that was my introduction to Alaska Ocean Products, or A.O.P. as it was often referred to, a game of catch in the parking lot, and a suitable introduction it turned out to be. This was to be my home for the next six weeks, six weeks of hard work, new friends and love sickness. Six weeks of twelve hour shifts, sleeping in a tent by the water, despite the provided accommodations, meager food and fresh cooked salmon, one passing crush, and one friendship that will last a lifetime, God willing. I learned a new business and became proficient at it and when I left I'd earned enough money to cover all expenses for my summer's adventure with some to spare.

My Frisbee playing partners took me in. They told me what was going on. Not only had I stumbled on the very place I was looking for, seemingly out of dumb luck, but I had arrived at the very right time. The fish may not run exactly on a schedule but the time periods during which they can be caught and processed does. These precious fish are cared for by a branch of the state government that attempts to ensure that a acceptable number will survive each season's catch and be available for the next time around, either themselves or in the person of their off-spring. The salmon season was still a week or so off, but I had arrived at

A.O.P. just as they were gearing up for the Halibut season. Who knew? At the foot of the driveway, before it opened onto the lot, was another simple plywood structure that I now learned was the company office. It was here I was directed to go.

And I did. And I got hired. Just like that I was employed. I must have looked the part, an able body, on the spot and ready to work. No questions, no applications, just a nod of the head. The halibut season would start tomorrow. In the mean-time there was a tacit understanding that I was entitled to a bed in one of the cabins. Maybe bed is too strong. At either end of the plywood boxes that served as cabins were two wooden shelves built into the wall. One of those was mine, along with the right to sit on the front stoop, and in our case the old car seat beside it. In the center of the sleeping cabins was structure devoted to food. No refrigerator, just a table, a sink and a stove. Beside the main processing shed was a bathroom with a series of shower stalls. So I had it all, a job, a place to live, all the amenities. By showing up in the right place at the right time I'd gotten myself accepted. I was in.

And it was quite a gathering of tramps and travelers I'd gotten myself in with. There was a small contingent of the prep school crowd, but we by no means cornered the market. Things were slow during that first week, halibut season being nothing like the real salmon season we were gearing up for, and there was time to knock about. There were three other guys already in my cabin, the two high school students from somewhere in California, and a heavy-set guy named Terry, who was a student at San Francisco State University. He, unlike myself, had serious ambitions to earn money for tuition. He'd done the cannery routine once before, and had some sense of what to expect.

Terry didn't move easily and he'd taken the lower bunk on the right-hand side. I was sleeping directly above him. He tended to toss and turn and mumble to himself. Being a pretty good sleeper myself, this didn't concern me too much. But one night, Terry really had some kind of a bad dream. It was deep in the night, maybe two or three in the morning, when, out of nowhere, Terry let out a full-throated scream. I mean he held nothing back. Awakened from a sound sleep, I reached my right hand down to the lower bunk, and took his hand in the dark. He held on to it for a minute, and went back to sleep.

I did move out to live in my tent, a short time later, and it had something to do with Terry's sleep habits, but in the mean time I started to get to know the other workers. Just behind our cabin, was another structure that actually had once served as a trailer or mobile home, nothing fancy, this thing was well past its day, but it did have a place for four people to sleep, two Israelis an Australian, and a young guy with long hair up from California. The Australian, Howard, had made

and saved more than twenty thousand dollars in the construction business and

blown it all on the road. There was a woman involved, but he didn't talk about her.

The two Israelis were there to accumulate capital, something hard to come by

living on a kibbutz. One of them was recently out of the army wanted to become a

painter. His name was Tetro, at least that is what he went by, and he wore a black

beard. He also wore his black hair long. He had a thoughtful pleasant air about

him. There was usually a smile, somewhere just below the surface. Like me, he

fooled around on a guitar. He was into Cat Stevens, *Sad Liza* in particular was his

favorite. If Howard was given to lying crosswise on his bed and staring at the

ceiling, I guess losing twenty-thousand dollars over a girl can do that to you, and

Tetro was trying to finger a G chord on his guitar, Gerry a long-haired guy from

California was riding around the grounds on his motorbike, a beat up dirt bike of

some kind that made more than its share of noise. Gerry was about nineteen and

had poor habits when it came to providing for his smelly work clothes.

"Not again!" Howard would call out, in his priceless Australian accent, after

finding Gerry's boots in a corner of their home.

But they got along. Most of us got along. Across the way, on the far side of

the cook shack, we didn't call it the "cook shack," was another cabin, an actual wooden cabin, with a couple of other A.O.P. employees I came to know over time.

Tom was a real hitch-hiker, a professional. He'd gone clear across the country, the lower forty-eight, four times. Some people play golf, some people play bridge or tennis, some people drink beer. Tom hitch-hiked. I never heard extensive war stories, but I don't imagine there were many bad experiences. You do learn patience. Tom talked about that. Sometimes a ride comes along, and sometimes it doesn't. It just isn't something you can control, to throw in a little Twelve Step jargon. He'd been to Alaska the summer before and took the season pretty much in stride.

Tom shared his cabin with a colorful bunk mate named Lars. Lars may or may not have had Scandinavian roots. I believe he came from a fairly conventional middle class American family, but upon finishing high school he decided to set off for the wilds of Alaska. Not that he really had any experience living in the woods. He just figured he'd pick it up as he went along. And from what I understand, that is what he did. He ran into some old timers, and through trial and error learned how to take care of himself in the wilderness. At some point along the way, he enrolled in one the campuses of the University of Alaska, Fairbanks I believe, and got a degree in surveying, which meant that he could keep doing what he had been doing, but get paid for it. During the summers, when the money was enticing, he came in and worked at A.O.P. Tom and Lars knew each other. They didn't need to talk a lot. They got along too.

Another cabin, beyond the Israeli's but also on the left, was home to two sets of brothers who had traveled up in style. They had driven up from San Diego in a van and they were living right. With the luxury of a van to move them around they had outfitted their summer home. You weren't walking into some wooden box in the outback, you were walking into a real living space with books and decorations and real food to eat. Two of the brothers were of Asian descent, probably Chinese, and they were named Darl and Devlin. Both had been there the preceding summer and they knew Tom and the other old timers. Darl was a prodigious worker who moved boxes of frozen fish with a controlled fury, and a calm demeanor. Devlin had a generous heart and always made me feel welcome. There traveling partners were also brothers from the San Diego area. Pete, the older of the two kept pretty much to himself. His younger brother Joseph was a large man who spent winters working for a moving company. All four knew enough to work nights. They were on the night shift of the freezer crew, and they tried to get me to join them. But I wouldn't have it. Working above the fifty-fourth parallel was quite enough culture shock for me, without adding further to the disorientation.

I was asked to join the freezer crew, and this in itself was an honor. One day, during the on again, off again work of the brief halibut season I'd been trying to improve my humble living conditions. I didn't have much, just the belongings I'd been carrying on my back, but it seemed appropriate to try and put them in some kind of order. Word got out that there was an ample supply of large cardboard boxes in one of the storage sheds, and that they worked well as surrogate drawers, a place to stow things under the bunks. I was ready to pick up on a good idea, so I walked over to the warehouse, the secondary metal structure that housed some of the supplies, but I didn't just go in. I was raised right. I saw Ned, a sandy haired, affable man who wore a tan baseball cap, and I asked him for permission.

"I heard they've got some extra boxes," I said.

Ned gave me a good look and paused.

"Uh-huh, there's plenty. You can take a couple."

I was about to proceed when Ned held my attention.

"How'd you like to work for me?" he asked, in his quiet, unassuming way.

I didn't answer, not right away.

"I oversee the freezer crew, two shifts, most people are working on the line," he continued. "It's the same money to start."

It seemed like a good idea, special treatment, increased responsibility. I didn't know a freezer crew from a crew neck sweater, but this guy seemed nice enough, nice enough at ask me at least.

"Alright," I answered.

"I'll fill you in." He turned and walked away. I went in the shed and got my boxes.

Halibut season had started from the very first day. The halibut, when it comes into the processing shed is a large fish, fifteen to twenty pounds. The work done on the fish is conducted in stages. It is brought off the boat and into the shed and headed. It is then passed on to another person who pulls the guts. Then came my turn, my responsibility along with eight or ten other guys doing the same thing was to wash out the interior of the fish using a small water hose and a knife. I had to try and remove all signs of blood, to leave it as clean as possible.

I launched into the task with enthusiasm. I had my head inside that big old fish scraping away. Brad had it right. There were no fish smells here. Everything was fresh and clean, flowing cold water, and firm, white fish flesh. Even the plant was cool and clean. There was a background hum of noise from the freezers off to the right and the flowing water. There was the occasional loud interjection of empty tots and stacks of fish being moved by a hand trolley, or the louder noise of a tot of ice being jerked around by a larger piece of machinery. And there was the general hum of human activity, of people working, not talking, just working, cleaning fish.

A day working on halibut lasted only six or eight hours. There just weren't as many of them. I punched in at a small office on the far side of the shed, and punched out when I left. I was getting paid, making real money for my labor, and there was satisfaction in that. And when I wasn't working, I decided to relocate. There were, in essence, two residential communities at A.O.P. There were the series of eight cabins, one of them being an old motor trailer, with the cooking facilities amidst them, but on the far side of the processing shed, was another living center, a center of tents. The tents were scattered, hither and yon, amidst the underbrush that led down to the water. The residents of the tent neighborhood still had access to the bathroom and showers. They could still use the kitchen and they could certainly show up for work. They had just decided, that they preferred their own tent to the confines of a wooden box, or should I say cabin.

This is where I decided to move. I'd carted my family's old two man tent all the way from New York. There was no reason not to put it to good use. Terry's middle of the night outburst had not left me entirely. That was also part of it. He was a pretty mild mannered guy during the day, but the prospect of being awakened at three a.m. by a screaming bunkmate certainly contributed to my decision. So, I moved out. I folded up my brown cardboard box, so politely acquired, loosely stuffed my cloths in the back and made a couple of trips over to the spot I'd picked out. A.O.P. was paradise. I do believe that. But if A.O.P. was paradise, the spot I chose was front and center, the featured accommodation, the top floor penthouse with the river view. Call it what you will, it was really something.

I found a grassy slope right by the water. This was still an off shoot of the Cook Inlet, but I was camped above any high-water mark. I had the location to myself. From where I pitched my tent, no other tents were in view. Just water, grass, small trees and shrubs and sky, lots and lots of sky, I was facing the west. If people associate working in a cannery with smelly fish, they also associate Alaska with long, summer days. This association is certainly valid. What many people from the lower forty-eight don't get is that the long, long days lead to long, long sun sets. We're talking hours here, from maybe six o'clock in the evening until eleven o'clock at night, an ever-changing palate of purples and yellows and oranges, merging and mixing in the western sky. And from my new home I had this view out front. Across the water and above the mountains in the middle distance was this dance of light and color.

Preparations were under way for the upcoming salmon season. On the appointed day, predetermined by the fish and game department, A.O.P would begin processing the fish. The old timers knew what to expect and they were gearing up. Darl and Devlin did me the honor of inviting me to join the night shift of the freezer crew. They painted a pretty picture. Night time work in general has less pressure, because supervisory personnel is not around, or at least not in as large numbers. You might work just as hard, but there are fewer people breathing down your neck. This, at least is the picture they presented, a close knit group of guys who knew each other, worked hard, and had fun. It was attractive. I liked Darl and Devlin as well, it all sounded good. In the end however, my more conservative side won out. Who's ever heard of going to work at eight o'clock at night and taking lunch at two a.m.? And wouldn't that mean trying to sleep at two in the afternoon? In broad day light? The whole thing sounded suspect, and I declined. I was on the freezer crew, and if that meant working days that would be just fine.

The last of the halibut had been cleaned and frozen, the plant was clean, as clean as ten workers anxious to stay on the clock could make it, and the metal tots were lined up neatly against the wall. All was in readiness. All was in readiness for the onset of the complete insanity, the controlled madness that was about to begin. In the mean-time I had three days off, a long weekend beginning on a

Tuesday, in which to occupy myself as I saw fit. I didn't want to squander it. I still had Homer on my mind, that mythical city on the end of the Kenia Peninsula, but this time I wasn't heading down there alone. I wanted company.

I walked into the defunct motor trailer behind my former cabin to find a traveling partner. Howard was still lying cross wise on his bed staring at the ceiling, his four days' growth of blond beard matching his tousled dirty blond hair and his faded, soft brown leather jacket lying across his legs. Tetro's bed was in the same end of the trailer on the opposite side. Quarters were close. Tetro was wearing a dark, plaid shirt in shades of green and brown and was holding his guitar, his right knee crossed over his left. He was looking at the finger board as he tried to arrange the fingers of his left hand into the appropriate chord. Every so often he reached out with his right hand to lift a joint off the box to his right and take a toke.

The two bunk mates greeted me when I came in, Gerry and the other Israeli not being at home.

"Jordan. How are you doing?" Howard asked, lifting himself on his elbows.

"Good Howard. Good," I answered.

I turned to Tetro who smiled at me. He was a little stoned, but he was a first rate smiler under all conditions.

"Jordan," Tetro said over the finger board of his guitar.

"I want to go down to Homer. Want to go?" I asked him.

And, just like that, he set his guitar down on the bed, picked up a sleeping bag that was on the floor and we walked out the door. No discussion was involved.

"See you, mates," Howard called after us.

Tetro and I started walking across the lot and up the driveway. We were both happy. I was a little better prepared, I had a tent, but the weather was warm, and the skies were clear. Are such experiences reserved for the young? Is spontaneity necessarily lost with age? Couldn't say, but the two of us were off for a long week-end to one of the unsung garden spots of North America, very north America, the small town known as Homer. We were going home to Homer, though we'd never been there before. That was the refrain of a song I'd made up on the trip down, although this time it looked like I might actually make it.

It was late morning and we stuck out our thumbs on the main road headed south. The sun was up. Once again I was hitting the road with the morning light, but this time I was traveling as a pair. And we were a pair, a couple of Jews on the last frontier. Granted Tetro was a lot more Jewish than I was, but I'd been Bar Mitzvahed. I'd been to Sunday School and I could make the motzie over the bread. I couldn't recite the Kadesh, not even with a book, but I'd been to services on the

High Holiday's for most of my youth. I had credentials. Tetro, on the other hand was a real Israeli, just recently out of his two-year stint in the army. He was a pacifist, or so I gathered, and had managed to spend his time in an office. I have no idea how observant he was at home but Hebrew was his native language. He lived on a Kibbutz and he wore a black beard, not a long black beard, but a black beard none the less. Certainly our common heritage had something to do with our connection.

But there was more than this. We were both in love with what we were doing. Tetro had a very practical reason for coming to Alaska. He was a painter, a serious painter, and he needed capital to get things going back on the kibbutz, to set up a studio, or buy supplies or organize a show, or whatever else painters do, unlike myself who was pretty much just screwing around. But we were both a little crazy about the whole thing, the outrageous scenery, the mountains, the water, and the ridiculous prospect of spending weeks working twelve hours a day cleaning fish. It was all too much, but it was all wonderful.

Rides came easy. We didn't need to talk much. We were going down to Homer for a long weekend, a pleasure outing, an excursion. We weren't scared about the upcoming work, neither of us really had any idea what to expect, but this was free time, a low budget vacation. There were no kids that needed to be put to sleep, no spouse wondering when we would get home, no deadlines or papers or exams, none of that, a couple of Jews hitting the road. It was a clear day, blue and sunny. Homer was just where it was supposed to be. A large green SAAB let us off on the top of a large bluff, almost a cliff that looked down into the harbor. Below us was the dark blue water of the inlet and a bit off to the left was a narrow spit of land extending out toward the mountains on the far shore. Picturesque? Certainly, but also magnificent. Tetro and I had the same idea, we asked the driver to take our picture. We'd been chatting, and he didn't seem to mind. And there it was, and may remain to this day in Tetro's picture collection, mine having been lost along the way. But it was recorded, an Israeli in a green plaid shirt, and a Jew from New York in a blue sweatshirt, standing on a bluff overlooking the tip of the Kenai Peninsula. We aren't smiling, in that picture, but we are both content, and a little moved to be part of such an experience.

We caught another ride, this time side by side in the front of a green pick-up truck that brought us down the hill and into the town, and a picturesque little town it proved to be. There was a central square surrounded by small shops, a bakery, a food market and a seafood restaurant. It could have passed for a spot on Cape Cod or maybe Martha's Vineyard. Behind the bakery on a side street was an art gallery that sold work by local artists, photographs, wood carvings and wood block prints that had a Japanese influence. It was an odd assortment, but it reflected the

neighborhood talent, artists who had come north for the summer and decided to

hang around. That June morning, I could certainly identify with the impulse.

Tetro and I walked into the food market, which welcomed us with the jangle

of overhead bells. A large white cat scampered out from under our feet, as we

walked past a tall display of local postcards. They may not have gotten a lot of

tourist traffic, but they were making the most of what they did get. We bought a

drink, myself an orange juice and Tetro a chocolate milk, and went outside to sit

on a low-lying wall on one side of the square. There was nothing much to do, we

were just sitting taking in the scenery, when a young woman came into view from

behind the bakery. She was carrying a small parcel in one hand and had a large

green knapsack on her back. Then, all of a sudden, out of no where, Tetro starts

calling out something in Hebrew.

I'd heard him speak Hebrew before, but this sudden outburst caught me by

surprise. He'd recognized the large green knapsack. This woman was a veteran of

the Israeli army, and even here some ten or fifteen thousand miles away from

home, they knew each other. So Tetro had called out,

"What town are you from in Israel?"

And the young woman answered, also calling across the square in Hebrew.

They stopped and chatted, catching up I guess on news from home, but what they said exactly, I have no idea.

Tetro and I had finished our drinks. We dropped the empty containers in a wire basket and wandered down toward the beach. If Homer had been my destination, the Homer beach held its own significance in my travel plans, and there it was, a long narrow strip of sand running along a dark blue expanse of water. And up and down the beach were a string of colored tents in bright greens and blues. There was an air of activity about the place as cannery workers on their off time quietly moved about, tended fires, and airing out sleeping bags. It was early afternoon. It was still early in the season, but the beach had a lived in quality. The spaces between the tents were clearly defined, the pathways marked. No one was in the water, nor would they be for the remainder of the summer. This water was far too cold.

Tetro and I walked quietly by the bay, the expanse of water separating the peninsula from the grand mountains rising up on the opposite shore, not far off. I chanced to glance off to my left, and much to my surprise, I saw a familiar face. Tetro wasn't the only one who ran into people a long way from home. But it wasn't someone from New York, it was the older sister I'd met on the second floor of the Anchorage Youth Hostel. She was walking back from some kind of bath room, evidently they had facilities here as well, with a peach colored towel

wrapped around her wet hair.

"Angela!" I called out, nudging Tetro with my right hand.

I walked over to say hello.

"Jordan," she smiled at me. "You made it."

"Sort of," I smiled as well. Tetro had walked up behind me.

"Angela, this is Tetro," Tetro fingered his beard and gave a bashful smile in

return. Angela stuck out her hand and Tetro took it, but he still didn't say any

thing. He could be shy that way.

"Come on," Angela led us along the sandy path toward their tent, an army

green, large domed affair a little apart from the community.

"Debbie and Jo are working," She ducked inside the tent and came out a

minute later without the towel, but wearing a pullover beige Indian top and a pair

of blue jeans.

"What are you up to?" she asked me.

"I got a job. Not here, I'm up at a place called Alaska Ocean Products,

outside of Kenia, Clam Gulch."

"Nice," Angela said. "Jo's not happy. She's thinking about going home.

Debbie's O.K."

Tetro was paying attention to our conversation, even though he wasn't joining in. We walked over to their cooking area, and sat down, Angela and I on a log and Tetro on the edge of a turquoise water cooler. Angela poured three cups of water from a five-gallon transparent water container, and handed one to Tetro and me.

"I lucked out," I started to explain. "I was headed down here, and my ride left me off and I just stumbled on the place. I think it's going to be fine."

"What's it called again?" she asked.

"A.O.P. Alaska Ocean Products," I drank the water and took in the scenery.

"Where are you from?" Angela asked Tetro.

"I am from Israel," Tetro answered, as though that accent could have been from anywhere else.

"Never been there," Angela said.

"It is a beautiful country," Tetro smiled.

Angela smiled too.

There were other cannery workers spread up and down the beach walking about alone, or in groups of two's, but everyone was pretty much minding their own business. They were all a little sleep deprived or just plain tired from having worked through the night. The Homer plant was running two shifts. Angela had gotten off at eight that morning, the same time her two sisters had started work. Debbie and Jo would be off at six, and for some reason, Angela was not working that night.

"You brought a tent," Angela commented, nodding toward my day pack and orange tent bag.

"Yeah," I said. "We've got three days, figured we'd stay at least one night."

I looked over at Tetro, who was fingering his beard with his right hand and looking about. He turned his head toward me and nodded.

"We'll have a cook out!" Angela said.

And that is just what we did. Tetro and I passed the afternoon wandering around Homer. We walked out to the end of the spit and sat on the rocks, the large boulders that had been placed in the water to protect the harbor, and we started talking. We talked about a lot of things including what we would do with ourselves at the end of the season. I wanted to hitch up to Denali Park and look at McKinley, or Denali as it was then known in politically correct circles. It's the largest mountain in North America and I thought it was worth seeing. Tetro was still planning on flying back to Tel Aviv. He had a house on a kibbutz, a whole life waiting. He'd been in the army for two years and he seemed genuinely ready to get back to domestic life.

But then he started talking about Howard. It seemed that Howard had big plans. He was going to push on the Far East. That's how Tetro put it, the Far East. It wasn't a matter of a specific country, Japan or Korea or China, it was just another part of the world. Australians are known for their wanderlust. It's some kind of rite-of-passage down there, to pack up your bags and set off into the world. Howard was a little older than the typical Australian back packer, probably close to thirty, which is well into middle age in back packer years. But evidently he was still with the program.

"He wants me to go with him," Tetro spoke above the sound of the water rushing into and out of the crevasses in the rocks. We were protected from the spray, which would have been very cold, but still quite near the water.

"Are you thinking of it?" I asked.

"Not really," Tetro called back.

"Maybe I'll go," I said with a laugh.

Tetro looked over at me from the side, his head partially turned, one hand on his beard, then turned and looked off at the mountains. I followed his gaze, and as they often did, my thoughts turned to Connie. What would she think if I didn't show up at registration? Wouldn't that be a shock. I could send her a postcard from Thailand, or Cambodia, with just a picture of a Buddha on the front. I wasn't the only one out there with a girl on his mind. It was going around. We were afraid to face them directly, so we went as far away as possible, and hoped to gain their attention that way. It went something like that.

"When's he going?" I asked Tetro, in a controlled yell.

"When the salmon season is finished, maybe earlier." Tetro's English was fine. He had strong Israeli accent, but he got the words right.

I certainly hadn't thought the whole thing through but I wouldn't rule it out either. Take my earnings from the summer and get on a plane with Howard, or maybe a boat, but it would be a long trip by water. It was an open question. Going back to school had its attractions as well. I only had two years to go. I could get the degree and then travel. That was a possibility as well.

"I'll ask him about it," I called over to Tetro. "I'll ask Howard."

Tetro smiled. He wasn't passing judgment on this one. We got up and started hopping boulders on our way back toward the town.

That evening we were back on the beach. Everyone was there, Angela and her two sisters, Jo and Debbie, me and Tetro. We were cooking eggs. Don't know why we were having eggs for dinner, but we were. Jo was the younger of the two sisters, other than Angela who was the oldest. Angela is the one who had been there the year before and she still was a little protective of her two siblings.

Jo had built the fire and it had fallen to me to scramble the eggs. She had a pretty good blaze going with a grating over it supported by three large rocks. So I start breaking the eggs into a metal mixing bowl they had, and the strangest thing happened. First the first egg had two yokes. No big deal right? It happens from time to time. Then the second egg has two yokes, a little strange. But that was just the beginning. I broke all twelve eggs and nine of them had two yokes. This had certainly never happened to me before.

But a lot of things were happening to me that had never happened before. I was sitting on the beach surrounded by a glorious range of mountains, at twilight, eating scrambled eggs with four friends. Twilight was just beginning. We were in act one of a six part performance that would last well into the night, almost until it was time for the morning sun to start coming up. It was fair to say that the sun was actually below the horizon for about three hours. It was working over time. For the time being, however, we were just eating eggs. Jo and Debbie had just gotten off work and would be going back in the morning, but they didn't look too fatigued. Angela had said that Jo wasn't too thrilled with the work and I tried to figure out why. She was a heavy set girl all of nineteen years old, with a lot of black hair.

She was talking to Angela,

"He did it again," she said. "He yelled at me."

Angela tried to be soothing,

"It happens," she said. "There's a lot of excitement, people can loose their heads."

"But he doesn't have to yell, at me," Jo came back.

Debbie looked up from her plate, but didn't say anything.

"Can't you just ignore it," Angela tried again.

"He doesn't have to yell, I mean."

Debbie turned toward me, she had dirty blond hair that she wore in a loose pony tail. She was a little taller than Jo, and a little older.

"Do they yell much up there?"

"Not so far," I said, as a scraped up the last of my diner with the end of loaf of white bread.

"Everybody yells sometimes," Angela continued. "It's human nature."

"But I didn't do anything," Jo wasn't that upset, but she was making a point. "I was doing my job."

Tetro stood up and walked slowly down toward the water, which was also toward the sunset, now displaying primarily shades of deep purple and bright violet, a striking combination. I walked down behind him.

"Maybe she would prefer working at A.O.P." he said quietly.

Tetro wasn't one to get overly involved in other people's business, but something about Jo's predicament must have struck him, maybe it brought back memories of his days in the Israeli army. I looked down at the sand beneath my feet. It was a combination of tan's and deep blacks, almost a tar like substance mixed in with the recognizable grains or ground up sand stone. I'd taken geology back at Cornell, a million miles away, on another planet, in another universe.

"Maybe she would," I said to Tetro.

We started walking back up the sloping incline back toward the row of tents. Deb had taken the plates off to be washed. Angela was lying on the ground, her back against the water cooler. Jo was leaning up against her. It was a moment made for a guitar and a little music, but we hadn't brought one along.

"Where you boy's sleeping?" Angela asked.

It was a good point. We hadn't pitched the tent. There was still plenty of light.

I looked over at Tetro who motioned to a spot on a grassy patch up on a rise.

"Over there," I said.

"Good eggs," Jo said. She did look a little worn down by the whole thing.

"Thanks," I said.

"Jo's thinking about going back to New Jersey," Angela said.

Evidently they had been talking too. Tetro and I nodded.

"I'm tryin to tell her," Angela continued, "It's a shock to the system, all those dead fish. You're just not used to it." She glanced down at Jo.

Tetro mustered his courage,

"Maybe A.O.P. would be better," he said quietly.

"You think?" Jo asked, sitting up a bit.

We were both new comers to the operation, but Tetro seemed to have some opinions on the matter.

"It is a small place. It is smaller and quieter," he said.

Tetro was right about that. We'd walked by the Homer plant and it positively dwarfed the operation in Clam Gulch. Debbie arrived back from the water spigot, which was not far off and plunked down on a blanket in the sand.

"What did I miss?" She asked.

"Nothing much," Angela said. "Jo is considering career moves. Teneck, N.J., or Clam Gulch, A.K."

"What about Homer?" Debbie asked.

"That too," Jo said.

The Homer beach had lived up to every expectation. There were tents of cannery workers spread out across it and mountains across the water, there were people living in harmony, as the lyrics to some song go. But on balance, I didn't think I'd done so badly in Clam Gulch either. The town's name might be some what lacking in melody – Clam Gulch was not chosen to increase the tourist trade – but in broad strokes, I'd done O.K. I had a tent. I had a spot by the water and showers and a kitchen to cook in, and when we made it back there would be work, plenty of work.

Later that evening, Tetro and I lay in our sleeping bags inside my orange two man tent. It was still light outside, though it was clearly after eleven o'clock. The light of the still setting sun filtered though the billowing nylon. The tent had been around, on camping trips with my father, week end excursions to the grounds of a family friend upstate or the Delaware Water Gap. This time it had gone a little further a field.

"Where does Howard want to go?" I asked Tetro.

"He doesn't say," Tetro answered. He lay flat on his back on an army green quilted sleeping bag. Evidently the Israeli army distributed more than back packs.

"I'd like to head over there," I said.

I heard myself say it. It sounded logical enough. It was a first step. I had decided to consider the possibility. Tetro turned over on his side and faced the wall of the tent.

"Good night, Jordan," he said. "It was a wonderful day."

"Good night, Tetro," I said. "It really was."

I lay on my back and studied the creases in the roof of the tent. If there was a rain storm, we were sunk, no pun intended. The tent was not pitched very carefully, it could have been stretched out more tautly, but it wasn't going to rain. I listened to the sound of the tent bellowing softly in the breeze. I listened to the sounds on the beach, young people laughing and calling out to one another. I listened to the sound of Tetro breathing. I think he was already asleep, and I thought about Connie. How had I gotten myself into such a mess in the first place? I don't think I really loved the girl, I was just stuck on her, stuck in a deep mud puddle so that so matter how fast I spun my wheels I only got stuck further. I'd been in love once, sounds pretentious for a twenty-year old to think that way, but is was true, and she'd walked away from me, but this was different. This was Connie. I'd written her two letters. What could be more romantic than that? A letter from an Anchorage youth hostel, a letter from a cannery in Clam Gulch, A.K, long letters in a conversational voice filled with details and adventures and the repeated use of the word, "anyway," and she'd gotten them. I know because I'd called her once on the phone.

Backpackers and long distance travelers, however responsible, are inclined to stretch the rules every so often, I believe, and a fellow employee at A.O.P., one of the high school kids of from California who shared my cabin had given me a calling card number. Don't know where he got it, probably from some other traveler, who'd gotten if from some other traveler, and it worked. Someone was paying for these calls. I have no idea who, maybe some corporation in Omaha, or a trucking company in Rhode Island, but the card worked. You punched in the fourteen numbers and the call went through, no dime required. There was a plywood phone booth, or maybe it should be called phone box, it had no windows, beside the A.O.P. office and one day after work I went in and called Connie's number in Berkeley. She answered the phone,

"Hello," The voice made my knees buckle, a little.

"Connie, it's Jordan." I was making every effort to sound put together. She was quiet for a moment,

"Where are you?" Her voice was conversational but over excited.

"I'm in Alaska," I said.

"I know that," She said.

"How are you?" I asked.

"I'm O.K.," she was working as a waitress at her brother's coffee shop and it didn't particularly agree with her.

There was a silence.

"Did you get the letters?" I asked.

"Yes!, both of them!"

"You going to be there mid-August? I'm going to come down."

"Yes," Connie said quietly.

The phone connection was quite good considering the circumstances, but there was some static on the line.

"I might keep traveling…"

Connie didn't say anything.

"I might not go back to school…"

Her room-mate came in the room and there was some noise in the background. Someone was waiting to use the phone box as well. The static increased.

"Take care, Jordan!" Connie called out.

I hung up.

That was before I knew about Howard's plans. That was before Tetro and I had our conversation on the rocky spit. But even then I wasn't sure. Plenty of people were doing it, making money and traveling from one place to the next. It was appealing. I walked out of the phone box and nodded to a co-worker who was all set to start working in the row room, the room where there took the fish eggs out of the fish. I walked back toward my tent, and I felt like a million dollars. "Candy's dandy, but liquor's quicker," and traveling five thousand miles away and taking up in the salmon business sure gets their attention.

So I lay there beside my friend Tetro, and eventually, I dropped off to sleep. By three o'clock in the morning the sun was back up, at about six thirty I was up behind it. A swim was just out of the question. This water was fresh off the glacier. The ice burgs melted a little and the run off washed up on the shore of the Homer beach. Tetro came out of the tent behind me, rubbing his eyes,

"Good morning, Jordan," he said, his voice groggy with sleep as he stretched his right arm far up toward the sky.

"Morning Tetro," I said.

We stood and looked at the water. I feel strangely inadequate to describe what we saw, other visual images of my trip are more clearly defined, but it was a striking vista. The morning sun was now at our backs and its yellow rays lighting the tips of the softly swaying grasses on the hills of sand. The water itself was dark, not in a forbidding way, but in a pensive way. The waves lapped gently on the beach and broke in a flurry of white foam. The mountains were there, as they had been since I'd hit the road outside of Anchorage, but here they were more rounded and subdued, still mighty, but more gentle as if they too were played out after their journey down the coast, and were preparing to meet the even more mighty and imposing force of the open sea that lay beyond.

To our left the beach extended toward the end of the spit, the southernmost point of the Kenia Peninsula, where Tetro and I had chatted the day before. Behind us was the pathway that led into town. Off to the right, a way down the beach was the cannery itself, its outline visible in the distance.

"You want to eat?" Tetro asked me.

"What did you have in mind?" I asked.

We didn't have much food.

"Let's take a walk," Tetro said.

I fished inside the tent for a t-shirt, pulled it on, and we started in toward town, toward the morning sun splashing in pools of yellow and gold on the brown sand and waving grass. The sky was clear, the light blue broken only by wisps of gossamer clouds purple in the morning light.

We reentered the town square, along with the crew of a fishing boat and three cannery workers getting off the overnight shift. The bakery was open and we each bought a sticky bun and a container of orange juice. Neither of us had coffee. We sat down on the low wall, not far from where we'd sat the day before and ate our breakfast.

"You think I interfered?" Tetro asked me.

He was referring to our conversation with Jo and Angela the night before.

"No. I don't." I licked the frosting from the sticky bun off my right pinky. I could hear the sound of gulls calling to one another over head, and in the distance the horn of a fishing boat setting out for its morning work.

"I think I did," Tetro nodded his head.

"She's got Angela to talk it over with. She'll make a good choice," I smiled at Tetro.

He looked at me, and polished off his container of orange juice. We strolled back toward the beach.

That day was a bit like the one before. Tetro and I walked around. Tetro bought a wood carving of a whale. I bought a scrimshaw pendant for a woman friend, not Connie, but by early afternoon we had decided to head home, back to A.O.P. Homer had been worth seeing, but there was a life awaiting us, and we thought we ought to get prepared. We found Debbie sitting by their tent and went over to say good bye. She had a book open on her lap and was looking out at the water. She greeted us when we walked up.

"Hey!" she called.

"Looks like we're heading back," I said.

"So soon?" she was a little surprised.

"It sounds like all hell is about to break loose up there and we figured we might as well be prepared." I laughed.

"Safe trip," she stuck out her hand, to me and then to Tetro.

"Tell Angela and Jo good bye," I said.

"Absolutely, I will," Debbie said

Tetro turned up the wattage on his habitual smile and nodded his head. We turned to go.

"Jo might turn up," Debbie called after us.

"We'll keep a look out," I turned back. "Couldn't really say it would be that much better, we're both new here too."

"Keep a look out," Debbie said.

"Absolutely," I said, and we continued down the beach in the direction of the cannery and the road back up the peninsula.

Tetro and I arrived back at A.O.P in the early evening, and two days later, the salmon season began. I don't think it is fair to say that the salmon were all waiting behind some large coral reef or iceberg or something and all decided to come swimming in together. Rather, there was a specific date when the fishing boats were allowed to start lowering their nets, and lower they did. The fish came pouring in, and with the fish began the process of cleaning and freezing the fish. That is what we were doing. In general terms, all the locations were called "canneries," but it was far more precise to call Alaska Ocean Products a cold storage facility, there was no cooking or canning involved, that may have accounted for the lack of fish smells, everything was cool and clean.

Inside the main shed, the work was divided into two general areas, the slime line, and the freezer crew. As during halibut season, the largest portion of the work force was concentrated in the slime line, the conveyor system for cleaning the fish, but with the salmon in the works, everything moved much more quickly. The pace for the entire operation was set by the headers, two brave, or reckless men who stood at the door to the shed on an elevated platform and began the process. They chopped off the fish's head. I never actually saw this done, but I know that the speed with which the headers worked determined how quickly the fish passed down the line. The slime line was designed to take advantage of the force of gravity, each station being positioned at a lower level than the one before. The fish were also passed in an L shape which took advantage of the natural shape of the building.

As with the halibut each station along the line had a specific assigned task, pulling the guts, removing the eggs, upper wash, lower wash, kind of like General Motors, but the workers used cold running water and small knives instead of wrenches. Work on the slime line was regulated by the clock, two hours on, followed by a fifteen-minute break. You stood there and did your job. The monotony was broken in part with humorous song, one favorite being "Slime is on My Side," sung to the tune of The Rolling Stones "Time is on My Side." Attire was also carefully controlled to offset the conditions, black steel toed boots, thick rain pants and upper rain gear in yellow, and double black gloves, a liner encased in an outer shell. Workers were dealing not only with fish, but also with a steady stream of very cold water, in a cold and drafty building. Even with this outer protection however, the jeans and shirt worn underneath could only be used for that one purpose and were set aside between shifts. They smelled.

If the slime line was characterized by routine, however good natured, the freezer crew called upon resources normally reserved for more creative activities. Freezer crew members had to be on their toes and prepared to adapt to changing circumstances. There were a number of different operations that had to be successfully completed between the time the fish reached the end of the line and the time they were loaded into the back of a truck, and these tasks could not be broken down into regimented assignments. Things had to get done, and the freezer crew had to see to it that they were. If that meant working right through break or even two breaks, so be it. You'd take a rest when you got the chance. It meant being able to shout above the sound of the processing operation when necessary and using hand signals when that was not possible. It meant volunteering for jobs you weren't completely sure you were capable of.

Things started slowly. The first few days we went through our paces and learned the routines. There were twelve of us on the day time freezer crew and as time past we gravitated toward particular jobs. Ned, the man who had given me permission to take a cardboard box, was the supervisor, but he was pretty low key. If things were getting done he didn't say much. The guys who had been there the year before pointed the way. There was one rule, "look busy." We were paid by the hour according to the time marked on our punch in card. The longer we stayed on the clock, the more we made. This system led to some very clean work areas at the end of the shift as everyone was anxious to stay on the clock and keep cleaning. But you had to at least look busy. There was no standing around just to stay on the clock, coil a hose, wipe down the glazing machine, something.

In short order it became determined that I was going to be working at the end of the slime line, along with two other freezer crew members I came to know a bit. One, named Fred, was up from Santa Clara, with his girl-friend. He and she were continually in some kind of crisis which he didn't talk about. Maybe that was why he didn't talk much at all. His last job had been counting peregrine falcons in a nature preserve off the coast of California. My other co-worker was one of the guys I'd encountered when I first walked down the driveway into A.O.P. His name was Larry, and he was the captain of the Oberlin College Ultimate Frisbee Team. I only saw him throw a Frisbee that first day, but he was pretty good at it.

At times, other people helped out, but for the most part, the end of the slime line was our responsibility, Fred, Larry and Me. We learned out way as time passed. On a simple day the line would run one species of salmon at a time. The most common variety was called pinks. The pinks swam together, were caught together, were brought onto the boat together, unloaded together and started down the line together. They came, however in various sizes. The pinks were not a large variety, varying in weight from four to twelve pounds. There were three women who played a vital role in the whole process who have not yet been mentioned. These native Alaskans stood at the end of the line, the foot of the L shape, and appraised each fish as it arrived. In one quick motion they picked up each fish by the gills and determined in a second or two, no more, which weight category it belonged in. Fred, Larry and I had to keep things ready for these women. They had to have a place to fling the fish.

The fish were going to be frozen, and the key issue here is that they had to be frozen in an absolutely flat and smooth position. It just wouldn't do to go freezing a bent over or scrunched up salmon. The fish wouldn't fit in the bag, would screw of the box and certainly wouldn't look very appetizing to the customer. So our job was to lay the fish out smooth and flat on the tray. The process began with building a stack of metal trays. The palate was the wooden base of the, a wooden square about three and a half feet on a side and four inches tall, on top of this went the first metal tray with a white sheet of plastic inside. When this tray was filled with clean, headed fish, another tray was added on top. After four trays had been filled a blank was inserted, to help with the ventilation in the freezer, then four more trays of fish. Each tray could hold eight to ten salmon, depending on their size. A completed stack was nine trays high with the wooden palate at the base.

Building one stack alone would not be too taxing. Things got interesting, however, when you consider that the salmon were divided by weight. That's what the three sorters did. They determined the weight of the fish and sent them flying off to the appropriate stack, two to four pounds, four to six pounds, six to eight pounds, eight to ten pounds and ten to twelve pounds. Right there you could have five different stacks going at once, each needing to be supplied with clean trays and plastic liners, each stack needing to be carted away when finished, each new stack needing to be started with a fresh palate. That too would have been O.K. But that was not the end of the story. Salmon species did not always come down the line one at a time. Two even three species could come down at once. Now imagine that whole process I just laid out multiplied by three, or even, on occasion four. Imagine three hair-brained workers trying to keep fifteen stacks going at once, three different species coming down the line, the sorters flinging fish off left and right at a furious pace, and Larry, Fred and myself running around like scared rats trying to keep the stacks going, the right number of trays, clean plastic sheets and fresh palates at the foot of each stack. Just thinking about it can fry your brain. And that is the way it was when things really got going. I went on automatic pilot. I couldn't think at all. I just moved.

It didn't happen all at once. For the first week the line ran one species at a time and the three of us began to feel our way. When the whole operation was up and running, it was really loud in the shed. We could only make ourselves heard at a yell, so we learned to anticipate each other's next move. This stack, the four to six's, was on its eighth tray, it would be needing a new palate shortly. Was one available? It was also going to need to be carted away from the work area, over toward the freezers. Was there a free hand truck? No one had been paying attention to the ten to twelve's, better get over there. There were already too many fish on that top tray, move.   Larry just ducked over to check on the four to six's. That should be O.K. You had to keep one step ahead, and keep moving. Tight abdominal muscles and readiness to make sudden movements were a plus.

To make matters even more interesting, sometimes we ran out of trays and plastic sheets. That meant that one of the species had to be stored temporarily in a large metal container called a tot, with ice. And what if there wasn't enough ice, and there was no one to get us more? Well, I once jumped on a large piece of heavy machinery and drove it down to the ice house, near the dock for another tot of ice. I very nearly tipped the thing over, not the tot, the piece of heavy machinery. But the fish were coming down the line. There was no way to stop them. What were the sorters supposed to do, fling the fish on the cement floor?

That was the freezer crew. That was how I earned my hourly wage. The shift started at eight o'clock in the morning and ran until eight o'clock in the evening. Darl, the younger of the two Chinese brothers who had driven up from San Diego, and I, developed a tradition. At eight o'clock am, when I was coming on to work and he was quitting we would pass at the door to the shed. I'd say "good morning," and he'd say "good night." The night time freezer crew had somewhat different responsibilities. They processed fish during the night as well, but at a slower pace. The head foreman was not around and they took care of some of the house cleaning we didn't have time for. They worked just as hard, I think, but nobody really knew for sure because the rest of the world was asleep.

It was about this time, two or three weeks into the salmon season, that I had another run in with anger, justified anger. I certainly had never heard or used the term, "justified anger," but that's what this was. I got very upset. I had just cause. I had a reason for getting upset, I just didn't know at the time that it was something I was constitutionally unsuited for. I also didn't know a lot about other things, including money. I'd headed north with something of a security blanket, thanks to the generosity of my maternal grand-mother. She had been ill at ease with the idea of my traveling alone to the last frontier, and had insisted on my taking enough travelers checks for a plane ride back, should the need arise. Somehow I don't think Davy Crockett or Daniel Boone had the same sense of security, but what could I say?

"No, I refuse to take your money!"

So there I was, working hard and making good money, but also carrying around a large wad of cash. And I must have told some one about it, first mistake.

That resource caused me some trouble.

One of the two high school kids who shared my original cabin was named Jaimie. I would say he was seventeen or eighteen years old, but he lifted weights so he had a substantial look. Jaimie wanted to buy a dirt bike. Why in heavens name should Jaimie's dirt bike have anything to do with me? That's the logical question. But at the time boundaries were not that clear. We were around each other all day and night with ample opportunities for personal conversation. Jaimie wanted five hundred dollars to buy his dirt bike, and he reassured me repeatedly, that if I loaned him the money he would pay me back. Any reasonable appraisal of the situation would have led to one conclusion. Walk away. You don't know this guy. You certainly don't owe him anything. You'll never see the money again. That would have to be the reasonable appraisal of the situation. But somehow, at the time, I didn't see it that way, I gave Jaimie the money.

He was persuasive. He explained that he really needed the dirt bike. He explained that he would pay the money back as soon as he got paid, which wouldn't be far off at all. And I had all this money just sitting in my money belt. What could I say? I gave way. I hadn't worked for that money or accumulated it through any form of toil. It had been given to me for a specific purpose, granted, still it had just appeared. It didn't seem like such a big deal to part with it for a while, and it would only be for a while. That's the way I saw it. The issue here is the person I was giving the money to. He just was not a very trustworthy individual. He wanted the dirt bike, on that he was clear, but everything else was a little shady. He wasn't on the freezer crew for one thing, and to make matters far worse, shortly after I made the bequest, he left A.O.P. entirely. He took a job at another facility, that wasn't even cold storage. It was a cannery where they cooked fish and put them in cans. I mean really.

So there I was three weeks later with an entirely worthless I.O.U. and a money belt lighter by the weight of five-hundred-dollars in traveler's checks. The cash was gone and so was the dirt biker, which is a kind word for the way I started thinking about the guy. He was completely gone. Gone from the cabin, gone from the lot, gone from A.O.P., and he had gone off with my money. In the grand scheme of things loosing large sums of money is generally the kind of thing people get worked up about. That money could translate into food or clothes, or evenings out, or a sizable addition to a savings account, or in my case a plane ticket from Anchorage, A.K. to N.Y.C. No small thing. There are courts set up to deal with exactly this kind of situation, created to prevent blood shed or loss of life. Given where I was at the time, however, small claims court was not an option. I got steamed up. And for me, at that time, getting steamed up was no laughing matter.

I realized Jamie wasn't going to pay me back. I realized that he had skipped the joint, with his new dirt bike, and moved on to other things. I was a little upset. Essentially, we worked seven days, but some weeks there was a day off, which was much needed to hitch into Kenia, do laundry and buy groceries. On this day off, I had other things on my mind. I found out the name and location of Jamie's new cannery and I was going to go over there and give him a piece of my mind. I had spoken to a number of the big thugs at A.O.P., the guys who cut off the fish heads, went to whore houses and generally raised hell, and they were behind me. They knew what Jamie had done and without going into specifics they let me know that they did not approve.

So I walked up the drive way to Jamie's cannery with a note in my hand that explained that he had better deposit the five hundred dollars in the bank account named below, my checking account in Kenia, or there would be consequences. So far, you might think that I hadn't done so badly. Apart from giving him the money in the first place, I was getting results, or moving in that direction. The problem here was my state of mind walking over to Jamie's cannery. It was not normal. I think it is fair to say that I had moved into an altered state of consciousness. Like my walk away from the topless bar in Anchorage, I was over the top. I was zoned.

I had taken a one-way trip to another place and time. My feet were moving over the pavement, but my head was somewhere else entirely. That is the nature of anger. I had no perspective on it at the time, but I was not acting in a manner conducive to my own health, mental or other was. I was in a rage. Not outwardly, on the outside I had a steely calm, but inside, I was floating up and away, buffered from the world by four or five feet of churning water.

I am pleased to say, the note accomplished its intent.   The next time I went into town, a few days later, the five hundred dollars was in my checking account. You can't take money out of someone else's account, but you can put money in. I'd given him the account number and Jamie had deposited the money. He'd been sobered. Maybe he intended to return it all the time, or maybe the thought of upsetting the A.O.P. fish headers didn't agree with him. Something worked. And I learned something about money. It's the kind of lesson you're not going to learn in a classroom. If money has been handed to you without punching any kind of time clock, it can have an aspect of unreality, until you lend it to someone who doesn't give it back. Maybe next time I'd be a little more careful, maybe not. I'd also had another run in with anger, but this lesson escaped me entirely. The thought that there had been anything abnormal in my emotional reaction to the situation never entered my mind. The guy had wronged me and I had set him straight, end of story. It would take years of escalating rages, mostly interior, before someone set me straight on that one.

Kenia was more than the home of the First Alaska Bank branch office, it was the place we went to buy provisions and clean our clothes, the clothes that weren't so smelly that they were beyond cleaning. The only mode of transportation between A.O.P. and the town of Kenia was, as usual, hitch hiking, but it was rarely difficult to catch a ride. The locals knew who we were and were generally sympathetic. None of them wanted these jobs. They owned the boats and went out and caught the fish, but they left the processing to the summer kids from the lower forty-eight, the notable exception being the three women who sorted the fish at the end of the slime line. This required real skill, skill you couldn't just pick up a week and a half. It required judgment and a keen eye. These women knew what they were doing. I got a crush on one of them.

I know it sounds like I was being incredibly unfaithful to Connie, and believe me, it didn't lead anywhere, but she was really a gorgeous girl. Her name was Estelle, she was about five feet eight inches tall, and man could she fling an eight-pound fish. Seriously, she was quite beautiful, a stunning figure, even in a plaid flannel shirt, deep green eyes, long flowing hair streaming out from under her red baseball cap. And she liked me. Actually she was friendly with me and a

Larry, the ultimate Frisbee captain from Ohio. It definitely livened up the day and I think I can say with confidence that in the beginning I was out in front, with Larry somewhere in the back ground. Here again, I made a mistake, that's what it was all about, remember? but here the mistake wasn't about money, it was about women.

We were on break and one of the older women sorters, who may have been Estelle's aunt or older cousin, was having a cigarette in the open passage way between the processing shed and the changing room that had the showers. She struck up a conversation.

"You like Estelle?" she asked as she exhaled a long flow of white smoke.

Lesson number forty-three, never admit that you like the girl.

My mistake, glancing at the ground,

"Yeah,"

The break ended.

I would not for a minute pretend that I've made all the necessary mistakes there are to be made in dealing with the opposite sex, but I can say that the next time around I didn't handle that one in the same way. It was not the right answer. Larry moved ahead of me in the game of love. He became the new favorite and even went out after work with her a couple of times. Nothing happened there either. Larry had his own problems. He'd come up to Alaska with his girl-friend who took up with another guy, and one drunken night the two of them drove off and left Larry in the road. He'd fallen out of the back of a pick-up truck. He kept coming into work and freezing fish, but Larry had plenty of his own problems.

Throughout all this there was the on-going necessity of feeding yourself. There was the kitchen which had a stove, but much of the time there wasn't time for that. I still had a bunk in my cabin where I could keep stuff, although I slept in the tent, and on break I would go back to the cabin and eat peanut butter and generic corn flakes, which may be what is now known as a complete protein. I didn't think of it that way at the time. It was simply a meal that didn't require a lot of preparation. On occasion, I did take advantage of the cooking facilities to prepare a real meal, Kraft Mac and Cheese out of the small box and a can of green peas. This meal required two pots and some boiling water. It also necessitated washing the pots afterwards, but solid nourishment was at times required.

The specialty of the establishment was fresh salmon, of which, as I think I have made clear, there was an abundant supply. It made for a fine and memorable feast. On a rare occasion, Ned would fillet a fish, and hand out steaks to a couple of us. Then we really ate. I can say, in all honesty, that one of the finest, best tasting foods I ever ate was fresh salmon, only hours off the boat, cooked over an open fire, in the tent neighborhood of A.O.P. I sat around a fire pit, with a

member of the slime line named Gray, with the ever present Alaskan sunset

painted on the sky and cooked the salmon in a pan. There was no grill, just the

sizzling of the fresh fish held over an open flame. And the taste was indescribable.

Maybe it should be featured on one of those television cooking shows that seem to

have become so popular. Pull salmon out of hold of fishing boat, fillet is less than

two hours, cook over an outdoor fire. Short and simple, no extra ingredients

required, just the way God rustled it up. It was a satisfying meal.

In the meantime, life in the freezer crew continued. I continued to hold

down my responsibilities at the end of the slime line, with Fred, the thoughtful

bird watcher, and Larry the stressed out ultimate Frisbee captain. We continued to

refine our team work, until we really did work together with very little need for

verbal communication. But the freezer crew had other responsibilities. Once the

three of us had completed our task, and built a stack of trays nine stories high,

eight with fish, and one blank in the middle for air circulation, the stacks were

wheeled over and placed in a large walk in freezer, hence the name "freezer crew."

When the freezer was full, it was turned on and those fish were frozen up good.

This took some hours. But there was still more work to be done. Each of the fish

had to be glazed before it was placed inside a plastic bag, stowed in a carefully weighed card board box and shipped out to restaurants, waiting to serve "fresh fish" to their customers, in the lower forty-eight. They only thought they knew what fresh fish was, having never dined in the tent neighborhood of Alaska Ocean Products.

This glazing process also involved a number of steps that like the slime line were arranged in assembly line format. The heart of the matter here was the glazing machine, a huge stainless steel affair, some twenty five feet long. The process began with a mighty crash. Two freezer crew members, standing on a raised platform at one end of the machine, hoisted a tray of frozen fish into the air and let it come hurtling down breaking the salmon off the plastic tray and apart from each other. These same two people then placed the fish in grooves on a conveyor belt that moved through the machine. While enclosed in the stainless steel passageway, the fish were sprayed with a liquid solution that I think contained corn syrup. At the far end five or six other freezer crew members were waiting to receive them. Standing on each side of the moving belt the crew member picked up the salmon, slid it in a long narrow plastic bag, and gave the bag a firm twist. He then placed the frozen, bagged fish in a large, brown card board box.

The final step was the weighing and registering, before the boxes were loaded into a large truck waiting outside the door. There was only one woman on the day shift freezer crew. Her name was Audrey, and she figures later in this story as she traveled north with us to Denali. At this time, her job was to see to it that each box weighed exactly twenty-five pounds. She took out slightly larger fish and replaced them with slightly smaller ones, or the other way around, until she had a box of the right weight. Then it was registered on a tally sheet, and carried outside. Audrey did other things when necessary, but the freezer crew was a fairly sexist operation. Many of the jobs, such as lifting at tray to the top of a stack, already seven stories high, did require upper body strength, that may have been part of it. There were women on the slime line but many of them worked in the room designated for collecting and preserving the row, or fish eggs. I never saw this room myself, but I gather it was a largely feminine operation.

When the slime line was down and we were all caught up, I helped out with the glazing operation. I stood at the far end and slipped fish into plastic bags, and twisted them shut. I never broke the trays myself. This sounds like a fairly tame operation, inserting a frozen salmon of between four and twelve pounds in a plastic bag and twisting it shut, but it had its own risks and dangers, tendonitis. Once the fish was inside the bag, the next step was to hold the top of the bag with one hand and give the body of the bag a firm twist with the other. There may have been other ways of going about this, but that is generally the way it was done.

This twisting motion tended to put a strain on the wrist of the arm that did the

twisting. When the motion was repeated four hours a day for five or six days in a

row, trouble could set in.

They had to put me on the disabled list. I was in good standing with the club,

so they didn't release me. They sent me to a rehab assignment, stapling cardboard

boxes in the warehouse. Across the roadway from the main processing shed was

another building, considerably smaller, that was entirely devoted to maintaining

the supply of cardboard boxes necessary for our operation. This was actually the

spot where my good upbringing secured me a spot on the freezer crew in the first

place. And that is where they sent me until my tendonitis could heal, or mend, or

do whatever wrists with tendonitis do. The warehouse was not a well light place,

wall to wall brown cardboard boxes, most of them in a flattened condition. In the

heart of this brown card board world was a standing stapler, operated by a pedal

that you stamped on with your foot.

That was my job, folding card board boxes into shape and stapling them

with this large pedal operated stapler. There was a guy in charge here too. I guess

there usually is. I have no idea what his name was, but he was heavy into southern

rock, Marshall Tucker, the Allman Brothers and others of that ilk. He impressed me as somewhat of a hard character, but that wasn't saying much at the time, myself being far from it. He hung out with the tougher crowd at A.O.P.. But the cardboard warehouse was his place, his lair if you will. We hung out there and stapled boxes. As I recall, I did most of the stapling and he mostly controlled the tape player.

It was a change of pace. The freezer crew got along just fine without me. Someone else filled in at the end of the line and the fish all got processed. And over time, my wrist healed. It was kind of Ned to treat me that way. He didn't make a big deal out of it. He just let me know that I should work in the box warehouse for a while. Every one took it in stride. But I think I can say that I was a valuable member of that team. Once the owner of the whole operation even commended me. The Scandinavian man who had hired me on the first day, just before halibut season, came by the processing shed and conveyed something positive about my work habits. I was pitching in. You might even say I was thriving. I also wasn't working in any way with knives, which had been a concern at the outset. All things taken together it was a pretty good report, for a college sophomore, who had started out in a library in Ithaca, New York, with nothing more than a wild idea of going to Alaska.

We recognized the symbolism, we residents of Ithaca. It was not uncommon to walk through the hallway of a Collegetown house or apartment and see a poem about going forth from Ithaca. The Odyssey was still required reading for most middle schoolers in the mid '70's, and we all had a general sense of where Odysseus had started out from. Our Ithaca, the one in western New York, had some mythical qualities of its own, being the permanent home base of a generation of aging hippies with greying pony tails, who had never moved on from their college days in the late '60's, and had generated quite a community of their own, complete with a mayor who proudly belonged to the Democratic Socialists of America. How many small cities in western New York State can make that claim? Not many. Ithaca had whole food, grain store cooperatives, and far more than its share of progressive volunteer organizations. It was also home to a recurring population of eighteen to twenty-two year olds who bought into the symbolism of its name.

Well I had indeed gone forth from Ithaca, and so far I'd had my share of adventures, and all things taken together, I was holding up quite nicely, thank you very much. I hadn't spent as much time with Tetro since our excursion down to Homer. He was on the slime line, working days, and I saw him in passing, but that was really about it. Then one day we had occasion to talk. Jo showed up. Just like that, without either of her older sisters. I saw her from the distance walking into the office to speak with the big man, and she got herself hired. Later that afternoon, I saw her again coming out of one of the cabins. She seemed happy to see me.

"Thought I'd give it a try," was all she said.

I guess the thought of flying all the way home to New Jersey wasn't that appealing. I also thought that maybe she had a thing going for Tetro, but I was dead wrong about that. Within a week and a half, she'd settled in and struck up a thing with Darl. I know I mention all these different guys in passing. Darl was the younger brother who had driven up from San Diego, and was living well. He was Asian, a hell of a worker, and greeted me every morning when I arrived at work. Well Darl and Jo really hit it off. They were pretty low key about it at first, but word got around. Jo was working in the row house, putting fish eggs in a small, wooden boxes, and when they weren't working Darl and JoJo got to know one another.

Talk about a romantic way to meet your intended, co-workers at A.O.P. in Clam Gulch, Alaska. If it hasn't come through already, I was filled with admiration for this Darl, and not just for his work habits and calm demeanor. One day he was laid up in his cabin with a bad cold, and being a good co-worker, I prepared some soup and brought it to him. He was lying on his bunk. There was something about their cabin. Maybe it had two windows instead of one. There certainly weren't any potted plants, but there were books and decorations. It was the home to four people who knew each other very well and respected each other's possessions and living areas. So Darl was lying on his bed taking it slow, and recovering from his cold but he wasn't just lying there. He was stretched out on his stomach coloring in the areas of a workbook of some kind.

I came over and he showed it to me. It was a biology work book, physiology I think, that had diagrams of all the different parts of the human body, internal and external. This just about knocked me over. Here we were on the last frontier, freezing fish night and day, and this guy is using colored pencils to teach himself human anatomy. I didn't make a big deal about it at the time. I gave him the soup, chicken noodle I think, and stayed for a short chat. He was back at work a couple of days later. But it just goes to show you, there is more than one way to get an education. And wasn't that what it was all about? Realizing that there is more to life than classes and library stacks and summer internships and even entry level jobs, that there is a huge, huge world out there filled with people doing things their own way, and even educating themselves in their own way. Darl turned up in Ithaca some years later, and got himself a Cornell degree in landscape architecture, but the fact that he was confined to bed rest in a cabin on the grounds of a cannery in Clam Gulch, didn't stop him from broadening his base of knowledge. So he didn't go into medicine. He used his time in a most constructive fashion.

My time was not always so gainfully employed. As I may have mentioned, there was an old car seat just outside the door to the cabin I still used as a home base. I was sleeping in my tent, and quite content there, but I still hung out in the cabin area, and I had taken to playing guitar on that old car seat. It wasn't much. An old off green thing, that once served as the back seat to someone's Chevy, or Ford Mustang. Now it just sat there and fended off the rain. It was positioned on top of a couple of cinder blocks so that it was off the ground, but for all intents and purposes, it was really just sitting in the dust and gravel. Hey, this was not the Grand Hyatt.

And in the Guthrie tradition I tried to write some songs of my own, one song in particular. Maybe it was also in the tradition of the Knights Errant, who Don Quixote was so hung up on because I wrote my song about Connie. I'm not saying it was a good song, probably it wasn't. It would never be played on a college radio station or even at a county fair, or summer hootenanny. This one was just for me. I don't even think Connie ever heard it. But it helped. It helped me to get out some of the angst and pent up emotion. It started like this:

In the hills of California, a friend of mine is sleeping,

In the hills she's laying down to rest.

But where I am up here, in northern Alaska,

The sun it's still shining, like a fire in the sky.

It went on from there, continuing with the image of the sun burning on the sky and missing the girl. It had a beginning a bridge, I think that's you would call it, and an end, and I played it over and over again.

On balance I would have to say that the location of composition had more to commend itself, than the song did. It was too moody for a Guthrie song, Arlo or Woody, it lacked the vigor of their work. Actually, it had a lot more to do with moaning. What can I say? I'm not a song writer, never have been, never made a nickel at it. But I sat there on that old discarded car seat, starred off at the endless Alaskan sunset and obsessed about this girl I knew in Berkeley, California. That's the technical term for it, "obsessed," and it's the flip side of the rage. If you allow yourself to go into rages, the obsessive rumination will follow, sure as the night the day. You can't have one without the other. I knew absolutely none of this at the time. I didn't even acknowledge that I had rages. As far as I was concerned, I was a college sophomore out for adventure on his summer vacation, and actively considering continuing that adventure into the fall semester. The idea that there was something wrong upstairs, something that would grow progressively worse in the coming years was nowhere in my field of consciousness. Had someone even suggested it, I would have taken him for a lunatic.

Pay day came around every two weeks, and it was kind of event. Everyone milled around the lot, holding their checks and ogling at the big numbers written on them. During the heart of the season, we made five hundred dollars a week, a thousand dollars for a two week pay period. That may not seem like all that much by Wall Street standards, but for unskilled summer work it wasn't bad. It certainly seemed like a lot to me at the time. I wasn't trying to make tuition, and granted it wouldn't have gone far toward paying the bill at an Ivy League institution, but it could cover the costs at San Francisco State College or any of the other public universities that many of my co-workers attended. For some it meant having spending money to see them through the year. For me, it meant that I was paying my own way, at least for the summer, which was no small thing, considering the experiences I was having.

There were sub-communities within the larger A.O.P. community. One of them was a sizable group of lesbians who lived together in a couple of large tents on one side of the tent neighborhood. They had one large open tent, and you could see them cooking and hanging out together. They didn't make an issue out of their sexuality. There were no conspicuous displays of woman on woman love. I think they just felt at home out there on the western edge of the Kenai Peninsula making a living freezing fish, like the rest of us. No one was judging them. No one was judging anyone as far as I could tell. One guy was getting pushed out of the back of a slow moving pick-up truck and left half drunk in the road. People might wake up screaming in the middle of the night, and others might well be wondering what the hell they were doing with their lives, but nobody really gave a shit who you wanted to make love to, or hang out with, or cook with, or anything like that. They must have felt at home, or they wouldn't all have been there in the first place.

One young woman, who was definitely gay, became somewhat of a friend. Her name was Lauren, and we hung out together for a few minutes by the wooden telephone cabin. We knew each other from around the place. She worked in the row house, and she was friendly with everyone. But that day, she was upset. I was sitting on the steps of the office looking at a package that had come in the mail when she came out of the phone box, or booth, or what ever you call it. She was crying. She came and sat beside me on the top step, and I put my arm on her shoulder, and she cried a little. I'm not sure if we said anything at all. After a time, we got up and walked past the processing shed and back toward the cabins, the real cabins where we passed our days.

I know the word "friend" has been redefined in the age of Facebook. But really, by no definition of the word does any one person have one-hundred-fifty-two friends. It just doesn't work that way. I still believe you can count your friends on one hand. So what of these people I came to know at A.O.P.? Tetro and Darl? Howard and Jo and Lauren? We haven't kept in touch. Many of them I couldn't look up on Facebook if I wanted to because I don't know their whole name. Do they fall under the definition of that elusive word "friend"? I still think that if I ever made it over to Israel, Tetro and I would pick up right where we left off. We did exchange letters, and nothing has happened to alter the relationship we established posing for that picture on the bluff looking over Homer. Does that make him a friend? I would like to think so. Darl and Jo got married and moved to Ithaca. I was their matchmaker. Does that create a lasting relationship? I called Darl's house in San Diego and got his brother Devlin on the phone, and tried to make arrangements for a woman I had gotten to know to come to A.O.P. the next summer. Devlin said,

"My house is your house."

Does that make him a friend? Even Larry the ultimate Frisbee captain sent me a letter from back at Oberlin, with himself sitting at the helm of a sailboat. That was certainly a friendly gesture.

We never had a chance to screw it up. We were together for a couple of months and then we parted. How fortunate were we in that respect? Never to have to look back and reevaluate? Never to have to "come to terms" with how we'd behaved and how others had behaved toward us. It was six or seven weeks of intense work and intense personal interaction, and then, for the most part, if was over. No reunions to avoid, no wedding invitations to push into a stack of papers by the refrigerator. Just two months of freezing fish. My behavior was no better than the rest, probably no worse. I'd done my job, written a lousy moaning song, and slept in a tent by an exquisite body of water. I'd stayed to myself, which may be, after all, the only way to go. This whole joining thing, is, in my opinion, vastly overrated. I'd tried it, against my better judgment, in moving into a group house in Ithaca. But Cornell is a very large and impersonal university, not an easy place to be on your own. A.O.P. did not share that quality. It was intimate and accepting, a place in which to walk alone in comfort.

My days there were numbered. Fish and game had a date marked on their calendar, and even before that date arrived, I would be up and on my way. Exactly in which direction I had not completely decided. I still hung out in Howard and Tetro's cabin from time to time, even if Gerry did leave his smelly work boots lying in the corner. Tetro and Howard had been working hard on the slime line, and like the rest of us had accumulated some money. Tetro would be going home, back to Tel Aviv, but Howard's plans weren't so settled. Once these Australians leave home they are in no hurry to return, and Howard was still tossing around ideas about moving on to the "Far East." He said it that way, "The Far East," he wanted to start in Tokyo, and go from there, China, Malaysia, Vietnam maybe Korea. The whole thing sounded a little vague.

"You don't speak those languages," I pointed out one evening after work. We were all physically tired, but still pumped up from all the excitement.

"Everyone speaks English now," said Howard, in his own distinctive brand of that language.

These Australians have a fearless air about them. Maybe it's because they seem so casual, "No Worries, mate," that kind of thing. He did give you the feeling that he could pull it off. Just wander into all those different countries, give the locals a friendly "hello" and sit down for a pint, or whatever size they serve their drinks in. The thing was, he thought I ought to come along.

"What about it, Jordan? What do you think?"

Thinking, that was my strong point, but this one had me stumped. "The Far East," "The Far East," it had a ring to it. I had the cash. I had the cash before in traveler's checks, but now I had the money I'd earned myself. "The Far East," and what about Howard, a bit moody perhaps, but who wasn't? Probably a good traveling companion, he was a big guy at least six feet, he ought to be able to stick up for me in a tight spot. And I was already half way there. Didn't planes to Japan touch down for fuel in Anchorage? Some of them? Well here I already was, a hundred and fifty miles south of Anchorage and a good half the way to Tokyo. My grand-father had been there many times. Bought cultured pearls, I was familiar with the culture, a bit. And what about those other countries? They had youth hostels didn't they? Wasn't it all pretty much the same thing? Australians and New Zealanders and women from New Jersey with backpacks sitting around the common room of a youth hostel eating Ramen noodles? How different could it be in Malaysia or even Vietnam? The war was over. The tourist trade was on the increase.

"When would you go?" I asked Howard.

Tetro had been lying on his bunk, he had his guitar in his lap and he was quietly strumming the chords to *Sad Liza*, not wanting to interrupt our conversation.

"Soon, right away, next week," Howard answered. "Things are about through here, aren't they?'

I stood up and paced the length of the mobile home. This was a big deal.

Certainly not something to be jumped into lightly, I had my education to think about, two years done already, and what would my folks think? They seemed awfully far off from up here. They hadn't been too thrilled about the hitch hiking, but they'd gotten over that. This would be quite a blow. Still, it all seemed like a great chance. There was such a thing as a leave of absence. I could write someone a formal letter, explain things in a factual way. In a very real sense, I was wavering.

"What do you think?" I turned to Tetro.

Tetro didn't seem to be thinking a whole lot. He wasn't high. Maybe he was just coming down after work.

"Why don't you go, Jordan?" he said.

"Why? Why don't I go?" I was a little steamed up. "Because I'm a student, that's why. Because I'm getting an education. Doesn't that count for anything?"

This quieted both of them down considerably. They weren't trying to run my life, really.

"Couldn't you go back," Howard finally said, "and finish another time." It has a certain sing song quality, the Australian accent, which is soothing, kind of like the waves lapping quietly at the shore line. Imagine a whole country of people talking like that. That would be something to see.

"Maybe he doesn't want to go," Tetro said to Howard. He still had the guitar in his lap, but he had stopped playing.

"Maybe he's just not sure," Howard answered.

"No pressure," Howard said to me. "No worries, none at all." And he gave me a smile.

But the season really was drawing to a close. It may have seemed like more but there were only a little over three full periods, about seven weeks of steady work. Then it was time to move on. The question here was in which direction. We really were a fairly broad community and there was another guy I'd gotten to know. We all knew each other. His name was Wayne and he too came from a fine academic institution, Bowdoin, up in Maine. Wayne had been at A.O.P. the preceding summer and had shown up for work at the last minute just before the salmon season officially began. He'd been working all summer on the night time freezer crew and we'd become friendly.

Wayne had a plan of his own. Maybe it was my idea, I'm not sure, but the two of us started talking about hitching north past Anchorage, and up to Denali park. This too was quite an adventure. Denali was after all the tallest mountain on the North American continent, not the second tallest or the third, the tallest of them all. We weren't talking about getting on top of it, just heading up there to take a look. Somehow or other, Audrey got caught up in the conversation and said she'd like to come along. Audrey was the day shift freezer crew member who weighed and registered the boxes, and quite a cute number in her own short haired kind of way.

So there it was, in stark contrast. Get on a plane with Howard, for Lord only knows where and skip the fall semester entirely, or merely stick out my thumb, head north, and hope to make it back in time for registration. That was the choice. The salmon were still coming down the line, and being duly frozen, but there was an element of finality about the place. People were getting ready to move on. Howard was not persistent, not in the least. He had expressed his interest in traveling with me. He'd kindly extended the offer, but that was about as far as it went. Tetro wasn't bugging me either. It was up to me, entirely. Wayne and Audrey were also happy to have my company. We talked about the plan from time to time, nothing to specific, just that we'd head up through Anchorage to the Park and spend a few days camping there. Then head home. There was some talk about going to a big music festival at Talchitna that was supposed to be taking place at about that time, an end of the season hang out for cannery workers. But that was a little vague too.

I haven't spoken much about the role of my folks in all this. They'd dropped me off at the airport in the maroon BMW, and wished me well, or gone home to take smelling salts, one of the two. It had to be a little nerve racking to see your kid fly off to Alaska with no definite job prospects, but they hadn't stood in my way either. Still, I went through this decision process more-or-less on my own. I'd sent postcards, they'd sent up a replacement address book when mine was lost, I'd even called to openly confess that I was getting around with my thumb, but that was about it. I had two fine options before me. I just had to choose between them.

Tetro caught up to me walking away from the processing shed after the day shift,

"Do you want to go, with Howard?" he asked, coming right to the point.

"It's not Howard," we had turned in our rain gear and gloves with Norma, the woman in the supply room, but I could still feel my wet jeans sticking to my thighs. I'd grown thoroughly accustomed to the calf high black steel toed boots. It was eight o'clock in the evening and there was a cross flow of workers moving across the lot, some turning in for the evening, others just starting their day.

"I know," Tetro said.

He did know. He knew quite a lot. It was just a choice I had to make or let it get made for me. Howard was pulling out in three days. He was flying out of

Anchorage on some kind of stand-by program he'd heard about. You weren't exactly sitting in the baggage bay, but they certainly weren't serving you any free alcohol.

"Tell him I'm still working on it," I said.

Tetro continued on to his mobile home that was no longer mobile and I pushed open the front door of my cabin and pulled the guitar out from under the lower right hand bunk. Funny thing that guitar, yes I carried it around, and it certainly helped me get rides, but it was also good company. You sit on an old car seat, in twilight, and strum some three chord Neil Young song, and it can kind of settle things down. I did want to go with Howard, to get on that plane and head east. The wanderlust was deeply rooted. When I was about eleven I tried to convince a neighbor to just take off and start walking, just for the adventure, just to see where we'd wind up. He went back inside and watched N.F.L. football, and I made it about as far as the local park. I did turn up one street I'd never been on before, but all things taken together, it wasn't much of an adventure.

This was a little different, a plane, a few thousand dollars in my money belt, a world of possibilities. It was certainly something to consider. And consider it I did. But I didn't make all that much progress. The decision just kind of sat there. People around me were moving forward, things were happening. I just wasn't participating. I was still holding down my position at the end of the slime line, lining up dead salmon on white plastic trays, trying to make sure they were smooth and that their tails didn't freeze together. I was still camped out in my tent in the tent neighborhood, on my own, but among my tent neighborhood neighbors. I just didn't know exactly where I was going to go next.

But the day rolled around. That seems to be one thing that remains resolutely beyond human control. The sun goes down, however briefly, and the sun comes up. One day ends and another begins. We just can't seem to screw up that progression. So one morning, Howard came out to my tent. He actually walked over to the tent neighborhood, which is not something the cabin people often do. I was lying in my sleeping bag, watching the play of the light on the flowing orange canvas above, the creases, forming and reforming, and listening to the sound of the water in the inlet, lapping on the shore line. Not a whole lot more was going on.

"You in there?" Howard called out, with his Australian lilt.

I got to my knees, I was wearing a pair of gym shorts, and unzipped the front flap. I stuck my head out.

"That would be a yes," I answered, as I squinted a little in the morning light.

"Pulling out today. Wanted to say goodbye,"

Howard was dressed for traveling, a clean pair of jeans, a button down green shirt and pair of light weight hiking boots.

"Doesn't look like you'll be coming along then," he squatted beside me.

"Guess not," I answered. I finished unzipping the front flap and stepped outside. Howard stood up beside me. He put out his right hand.

"Be seeing you," he said, giving me a good look.

"Be seeing you," I said, and gave his hand a firm shake.

Howard turned and started back toward A.O.P. proper. I watched him until he was out of sight, his body hidden by the tall green underbrush.

Well, there it was. So much for the Far East, the Far East was just going to have to go on without me. A vision of the Uris Library seventh floor stacks flashed across my mind.

"What have I done?" I thought to myself.

I had a one way plane ticket to Tokyo, and I'd turned it in for a seat in a darkened library.

"Brilliant move," I thought.

But there she was again, my constant traveling companion, the woman of my dreams, who remained resolutely out of my arms, Connie, who had been up for hours and was probably already serving up the cups of hot Berkeley coffee to the morning patrons, anxious to settle in and read the morning paper. It was another story to tell. Not a bad one, about the time I almost left for Tokyo. It could be embellished a little, but it had potential. I headed off to a quiet part of the neighborhood to relieve myself, alone, and begin the day, the second to last I would spend at A.O.P., Alaska Ocean Products. The salmon season would continue for another week or so, but I was moving on. I wasn't going to Japan, or Vietnam or even Korea, I was traveling strictly by land, north to one of North America's greatest treasures, its northern most national park, to see the great Denali.

Wayne and Audrey were all set to go, and they really did welcome my company. We were a threesome which is, often a tough way to go, but at least at the beginning we got along just fine. We knew each other well enough, all three of us being freezer crew members, and speaking strictly for myself, I was not in the hunt for Audrey, maybe it was the short hair. She just never struck me that way. Wayne was an amiable enough guy, who generally walked around with a smile on, and a laugh not too far behind. All three of us had lives, or a sort, to return to. So for a couple of weeks we'd be traveling partners. It wasn't such a big deal.

Neither were the goodbye's. People were filtering out in groups of two's and three's, or entirely on their own. The salmon season was ending. The last couple of days they didn't run a full load, just the remainders. A few people had signed on to hang around and help shut things down. I was not among them. There was plenty of general conversation about where to go next. The word was that there would be more work on Kodiak, a large island off the southern end of the peninsula. Another species of fish was still being caught and processed. Details were a little vague, but the idea was that if you were interested, you could still make more money. Kodiak was also known for its extensive bear population. I'd decided to pass.

We left A.O.P. before Tetro. I don't even recall the last time I actually saw him, or what we said in parting. Tetro and I exchanged addresses, with a promise of mutual hospitality in either New York City or Tel Aviv. We shook hands. That was about it. What more could you say? Really? How often do you meet up with another person who becomes a friend so quickly and easily? No posturing. No feeling each other out, or looking for the higher ground, just two Jewish guys a long way from home, who happened to hit it off. But that was it. The season was over. Tetro was a painter, freed from the restraints of the army, and he was going home to paint. I was a student, and I was going home to study.

There were things that had to be attended to first, like getting home. I was quite a ways off, and there were a few things I wanted to do on the way back.

First there was the matter of Denali Park. I'd looked at the pictures a million times, and I wasn't going to miss it. Then there was the minor issue of a girl named Connie. I wasn't going to miss her either. I called. The call was brief, but I told her I was heading back to school. She sounded relieved. I also told her I would swing through town on the way back. This brought on a moments silence. I'd made an impression. I promised to keep in touch on the trip south. That calling card was still working. No one had blocked it.

So early one morning we headed out, Wayne, Audrey and myself, kind of like three turtles, carrying their homes on their backs we walked together up the driveway that led from A.O.P. back to the road, the road that led from Kenia down to Homer, except this time I was going the other direction. We started out hitching together, three people, two guys and a girl, but that didn't last long. Three people, each with a backpack is a lot to load into a single car. They all passed us by. So we split up. Maybe I was being generous, or maybe I already sensed something was in the wind, but I volunteered to go it alone, alone already being one of my strong suits.

We met up at strategic points along the way, to chart the next leg, buy supplies and generally pow-wow, and in the course of one long days travel we'd made it through Anchorage and up to the park. I took the final leg of the trip in the back of the open bed of a pick-up truck, just sitting there with my back against the sidewall, feeling the wind rush by my face. I totally get it that the in thing these days for upwardly mobile college students is to take internships in offices and learn how to program internet web pages, but without appearing pushy, I would like to put in a good word for sitting in the back of a pick-up truck as it winds up a two lane road toward Denali Park, late on an August afternoon. Granted, it may lack something on the resume page, but it is quite an experience none-the-less.

Wayne, Audrey and I met at the gate to the park. They'd arrived before me, but not by much. They were seated in front of the ranger station, the main receiving building just inside the park entrance. Wayne was lying on the ground, his head on his pack, and Audrey was lacing her boots when I walked up.

"Good trip?" Wayne asked, sitting up.

"Fairly outrageous," I answered. "Didn't have any long waits"

"Neither did we," Audrey said.

They'd looked around and found a place for us to spend the first night, in a camping area, right there by headquarters. Alaska really is magnificent country, everything the picture books make it out to be, complete with the wild moose wandering just outside the town of Kenia, I have neglected to mention. But up there, in the park, things took on an entirely different dimension. Huge, awesome, awe inspiring, those are just some of the words that quickly lost their meaning. The air was cool and light and on all sides were the most tremendous mountains. Gigantic masses of rock and snow thrusting way up toward the sky. Shapes, greens, whites, black rock, dark evergreens, one after the other, piled up in such a manner that it actually left you a little breathless just to look at them. You almost didn't even belong there. These mountains were just too big, too great for mere human beings to be associated with. But there we were, three cannery workers from Clam Gulch, and we meant to hang around for a few days.

It was getting on toward the end of a long day, and it was time to settle in for the night. We had company, an assortment of tents and RV's spaced out over an enclosed area not far from the ranger station. In many ways the campground resembled one you'd find anywhere in America on a mid-August weekend, mothers spreading out dinner under an awning attached to the front of a large, white mobile home, kids milling about, one on a bicycle. But there were signs that this was not Santa Barbara or even Wyoming. There were still those glorious mountains ringing the campground on all sides. In addition to the RV's hooked up to their sources of power and water there were a motley assortment of tents, inhabited by a motley assortment of campers. Music came from an adjoining camp site, as we pitched our tents for the night. Wayne and Audrey shared a tent. You'd think I might discern a pattern forming here, but I wasn't quick to jump to conclusions.

Early the next morning we struck camp, reattached our tents and sleeping bags to our packs, and went to make inquiries. There were procedures in place, both for the protection of the campers and the wildlife. It was possible to venture into the interior of the park, but it had to be done according to park regulations. The park was divided into regions, and the park service controlled how many campers were permitted into each region each night. This prevented the grounds of the park from being overused and also ensured a relatively undisturbed back country experience for the backpackers who were permitted in. We discussed our plans with one of the rangers and laid out a four-day itinerary for ourselves. If the number of hikers in the park was strictly controlled, the number of passenger cars was even more tightly regulated. The only vehicles allowed to travel over the park road were large red buses that stopped intermittently on their way to Wonder Lake at the innermost point of the road transportation.

We would start out on that bus, get off in our region and begin our hike. Bears were a real concern in Denali Park, and not just your every day average black bear of the kind you might run into in the Adirondacks. These were the real thing, grizzlies, and as long as you were inside the bus they provided a nice photo opportunity. The bus driver would announce the presence of one of our esteemed neighbors off to either the left or the right, and all the tourists would dutifully move to either the left of the right and take a picture. Whether the large brown object in view was actually a bear or a large rock, was of little consequence. We were all up in Alaska, and having a grand time.

The three of us, Wayne, Audrey and myself, had larger more authentic plans in the works, and at the appropriate stop, we stepped off the bus and watched it disappear around a bend. That was a lonely feeling, for we were quite alone, in the quiet of a vast, vast park, with only the predetermined number of other campers in our region, who were certainly nowhere in sight. We hoisted our packs, crossed the road and began to hike. We had a map, and a visual destination in sight. We were headed toward the cleft between two of the minor peaks off in the distance.

There is a brand of environmentalism that likes to speak about our commonality with other living things, that the earth is one home that we all share. This philosophy may not go very far on the eighty-sixth street crosstown bus, where there are no other living creatures in sight, save for a couple of scared pigeons, and institutionally planted trees carefully confined to a four by four-foot square of concrete with a hole strategically placed in the middle. This was

anything but the case walking across the tundra of Alaska's Denali Park. I do

actually think it was tundra. For much of the year it was buried under many feet

of snow and ice and during the last few weeks of August, it had the spongy

consistency of three feet of pliable foam. All was green and alive, and there were

no human beings around but the three of us, walking along with all of our

possessions strapped to our back. There was really nothing to differentiate us

from any other living creature that might have happened along, say a caribou, or a

bear. We walked along upright, on two legs, other than that it was all about even.

The trip had been mapped out with the consultation of experts, park rangers

who knew the back country intimately. We were going to spend two nights out

there, and had brought along enough provisions to see us through. We had a map,

and at least a general sense of where we would be going. No, we weren't planning

on summiting Denali, but we would get a pretty good look at her, without a bus

window in front of us, or forty-five other tourists clicking away at our side. That

first day, we took a pretty good walk, across a broad expanse of open tundra, if it

really was tundra, and up the cleft between two minor peaks. They were minor in

comparison to the enormity on all sides but the elevation had us winded none-the -

less. Yes, hustling between twelve of fourteen stacks of salmon was a work our, but it was nothing compared to this.

It was at the highest point of that climb that we had our first sight of what would become our regular hiking companions, the caribou. On the first sighting there were just three of four of them grazing on an incline off to our right. We surprised them. They looked up, froze for a minute, and then briskly trotted down the mountain side and out of sight. They wanted as little to do with us as possible. We paused frequently and drank plenty of water. It was a clear, sunny day, blue sky with large billowing white clouds floating by overhead. I should mention here that there was a social dynamic taking place that had very little to do with the glory of our surroundings. It had to do with three people hiking together, two guys and a girl. I wasn't focusing on it, or analyzing the root of the problem, but on some level I was not completely at ease.

I'd not known either Wayne or Audrey all that well before we left A.O.P., and we'd been on perfectly friendly terms, but maybe I was starting to feel a little left out. The ride up had been fun. We'd met up in Anchorage to do some food shopping and I mistakenly thought the animals we might run into in the park were called cantaloupes. I don't think I thought they were really called cantaloupes, but that is the way it came out, so everyone had a laugh over that. Maybe it was at my expense but I wasn't keeping score. We'd bought some Monterey Jack cheese, and crackers and fruit, everything we thought we would need for our visit to the park.

As night came on, we dropped down the far side of the cleft, and pitched our tents in a grassy clearing. That was it, just the three of us. There was no one else around. The backcountry regions were large, and the park service limited the number of campers to four a night. It was just us and the caribou, and whatever other of God's creatures might happen to stop by. After dinner we carefully placed all food related items in a large bag, food, plates, silver, anything that had even remotely come in contact with something even smelling of food, even the toothpaste. Everything went in, and the bag was hung from a horizontal limb of a mid-sized pine tree. This is a precaution taken by even weekend hikers in the Adirondacks, but up there, with those telegenic grizzlies hulking about we certainly weren't taking any chances.

Sleep came easy, after the day of strenuous exertion in the wide-open spaces. We had two more full days ahead of us. The mountain itself, Denali, was a constant presence, but unfortunately its outline was generally covered with clouds. You knew it was there, off in the distance, its huge mass bulking up toward the sky, but for same reason better understood by meteorologists it remained enshrouded by a blanket of grey clouds. The caribou were also a constant presence, roaming about in groups of three's and four's, sometimes more. These were magnificent animals, standing some eight feet tall at the tip of the antlers. They were muscular, and extremely sure footed, able to scamper up and down mountain sides that could only have been negotiated with extreme care by their clumsier two footed friends. They had very little interest in us, and when they saw us wanted nothing so much as to get out of sight.

That second afternoon, we split up. Audrey and I took a hike together and Wayne set off on his own. We were planning on returning to the same campsite we had used the night before, so there was very little chance of our missing each other entirely, and there was certainly enough harmony in our little group for this arrangement. Wayne returned flushed with excitement from his day's outing. It seems he had found himself in a tight spot, on a narrow ledge, some hundreds of feet up, with nowhere to go but forward. There are times like these you also don't find in urban life, where you feel yourself entirely alone and in danger. Wayne was hiking alone in a remote section of the park with no one to even hear him if he called for help. Yes, there are dangers living in a big city, but none like this.

That night as Wayne and I lay on the ground, having finished our evening meal, we had a remarkable Denali Park moment. It was about eight o'clock and still quite light out. The thing is, we had still never actually seen the mountain, the

Big Kahuna, the main attraction. It had remained resolutely enshrouded in clouds

during our entire visit. But this was to be no more. As we lay there, our heads

resting on a large log, looking down over a magnificent valley, the clouds around

Denali lifted. As if on cue from some celestial stage manager the cloak of white

and grey dissipated and the mountain itself came into view. There were still tinges

of pink and purple in the sky, and there she was. I'm quite certain it was a she,

and not only because of her coy behavior. There she was, the grand old lady, the

tallest mountain on the North American continent displayed in all her glory.

Wayne and I didn't say much. We just kind of took it in, and marveled at

our good luck,

"Worth freezing fish for?" Wayne said.

"Absolutely," I said.

"But that was pretty fun too," I added.

"Uh, huh," Wayne laughed.

There had been a certain sense of relief the last time I'd gone to punch out, as if, in

some respects, I'd made it through an ordeal. But this moment, lying there before

Denali was indeed sublime. I think that is the way the word is used by a school of

intellectuals, "sublime," for an experience so wonderful, and mighty, that it

transcends words, that it reminds you of another level of existence entirely. I'd taken a course in European intellectual history with a professor who was particularly fond of that word. He was also fond of a lot of three and four syllable words, and stringing them together into sentences that seemed to be saying a lot, but you weren't sure exactly what.

It was certainly an experience to be reckoned with, and certainly fodder for some great thinker, but at the time, all we could really do was lie there and gaze at it. Audrey came walking up behind us and sat on the end of the log. She too appreciated the view. And the show stretched on and on into the evening and into the night, as the light around the mountain gradually faded, never turning completely dark, before it began to become light again. But by that time the three of us were already fast asleep, a day mucking around in the mountains will do that to you, absolutely no artificial sleep aids required.

The next day was to be our last full day in the park, and we struck camp and once again loaded our equipment and provisions on our backs. We had a rough route mapped out for ourselves, ending with a bus ride back to the park entrance. Those red buses were instructed to stop for hikers along the route and transport them up or down the line. But there was still some uncertainty here. The three of us had discussed traveling over to Talchitna, for the end of summer music festival that was scheduled, and Wayne and Audrey were pretty excited about the idea. I, on the other hand, had my mind set on moving south and eventually east back to New York. I was up against a reality, and that reality was fall term registration. I also had Connie on the brain. I wanted to see her and I knew just where she was. It was just a matter of getting there.

We got an early start and took a route that led us along a high ridge. Once again, there were no other hikers in sight, but we did have plenty of company, the caribou. At first they only appeared in small groups, families of three and four but all that was to change. I was hiking alone well ahead of Wayne and Audrey who were strolling along and chatting, and alone I reached the crest of what turned out to be a large bowl, no doubt carved out by some prehistoric glacier. I reached the edge of the bowl and looked over the line of rocks the lined its rim, and within I saw a most remarkable sight, forty or fifty caribou standing in a group quietly eating their breakfast. There they all were grazing amidst the late summer grass and the patches of snow.

They immediately sensed that there was something there that was not a caribou, and they did something caribou do, and have probably done for time immemorial, they circled up, women and children in the middle and the males around the edge of the ring with the horns down, like some scene out of a wagon train in the Wild West. They were prepared. But there was nothing there. Just little old me, a salmon canner from Clam Gulch, hunkered down behind a large

rock, looking on. And for a while we stayed just like that. The caribous weren't

moving, not at all, and neither was I. Above and beyond was a clear blue sky, the

sun was shining, and the large white clouds were passing slowly over head. But at

this particular spot, on this particular mountain ridge, things were standing still.

Wayne and Audrey were approaching, slowly at a meandering pace, and

they sensed that I was looking at something. I motioned for them to keep quiet

and they swung around to the right, assuming another position on the crest of the

bowl, and peered in at the spectacle within. And believe it or not, that was the last

time I ever saw them. They sat and looked for a few moments and then kept on

hiking. The caribou remained still as statues, circled up in their defensive posture,

and Wayne and Audrey moved on. We had made no definitive plans about how

the day would end, saying only that I was thinking of heading over toward Haines

Junction for the ferry to Seattle, and that they were still thinking about going to the

music festival. So that was it. They kept walking I remained still. There was no

ill feeling here. I got a letter from Wayne a few months later explaining his

growing feelings for Audrey at the time and remembering how they had left me

"in love" with a large herd of caribou. I would have written back, then or at some

other time, but I never did find his address.

Don't know exactly how those caribous make decisions, but someone must have given the sign, because at what seemed like a predetermined moment, the entire herd turned and trotted briskly down the mountain side, out of the bowl, over a lip, and out of sight. The show was over, and as they disappeared out of sight, leaving the vacant landscape before me, I realized it was time for me to be moving on as well. Somehow, I had to move myself from this position, alone, in the middle of Denali National Park, across a good thousand miles of Alaskan roads, onto a ferry to Seattle, and down the California coast to San Francisco. I sat for a moment and examined the sand between the cracks of the rock on which I was sitting, the product of an igneous uplift millions of years ago. The small pebbles in shades of brown and maroon, sifted between my fingers. The rock itself was weathered but still firm and strong. It seemed like a long way to go, but there was nothing to do but up and have at it.

I began my descent toward the park road, the life line ferrying tourists and hikers alike from one destination to the next, with its red buses moving slowly along at the appointed hour. I was more cautious on the way down, taking an extra second to make sure my hiking boot was planted on the loose rock before transferring my weight. A slip, or a twisted ankle out here alone, could have been real trouble. I paused to drink water and eat some raisins.

"No point in getting overly tired out. Got to look out for myself," I thought.

I made it down without any mishap, and before long was seated in a window seat of the Kodak goldmine, jogging along toward the park entrance. My worn, un-showered appearance attracted the attention of some of the younger tourists, not too embarrassed to stare, and before too long, I was stepping off the bus, back in what passed for civilization in this part of the world. It couldn't have been much past one thirty. The day was still young.

I stopped into the ranger station to check out, as the procedure warranted. They liked to know that the same number of campers had exited the back-country regions as had gone in.

"All's well?" the female ranger gave me a smile.

"So far so good," I replied.

"We saw your friends," she continued, "They said you ran into some caribou."

"Absolutely! At least fifty, all standing together," I said.

"Good to hear it," the ranger closed the log book.

She opened the back room of the station and let me pass through to pick up my guitar, which was right where I'd left it, in the cool shade of the wooden room, amidst the other prized possessions of hikers, too heavy or cumbersome to be carried along.

"Come see us again," she closed the door.

"That would be great," I wanted to shake her hand, but I refrained. I passed out of the ranger station, and started up the road toward the park entrance.

I stuck out my thumb and the first four RV's past me by. The kids starred out the window, from two stories up, but no one even slowed down. My plan was to head north up to Fairbanks, and then hang a right and go east. There are actually very few paved roads in Alaska, so there weren't all that many choices. My destination was the town of Haines which rests on a body of water contiguous with the city of Seattle. There is a ferry that leaves once a week for the spectacular journey south, past ice bergs and other scenic features used to sell two week Alaskan cruises. Only the passengers on the ferry aren't housed in any kind of state room. They are just lying on the deck for a solid week, sleeping and eating, and watching the world go by. It sounded just great. The only problem was that I had to get there.

There was an element of pressure here. The ferry's departed, going south, only once a week on a Monday, and it was now Friday, mid-day. That did not leave a whole lot of time. In fact, that whole plan was in some ways quite unrealistic, but I was determined, determined and hopeful, a couple of good long rides, and I thought I could just about pull it off. My first ride came, surprise, surprise, in the back of a pick-up truck. If I haven't made it clear already, there are certain inherent reasons why a pickup truck is more likely to stop, first and foremost being that the driver can signal for the hitch-hiker to hop in the back and thereby avoid any direct conversation. The additional reason may have something to do with the people who buy pick-up trucks in the first place, but that is a little harder to pin down. Add to this that there are a lot of pick-up trucks in the state of Alaska and you start to get the picture.

But I had a ride, on a major highway headed toward Fairbanks. Fairbanks too has an aura of romance about it. It could be Jack London, or the guy who wrote the poem about the cremation of Sam McGee, one of those Alaska writers who went mushing with their dogs over the Dawson Trail. Don't know what happened to the Dawson Trail either. Sounds to me like a ripe opportunity for the tourist trade.

"Two weeks, all expenses included, mushing over the Dawson Trail!"

Well that was not my line. I was just sitting there, once again with the wind rushing through my hair and traveling over some pretty substantial highways, headed into a pretty substantial city. I didn't want to actually go into Fairbanks proper and see the sights. I just wanted to pass around the edges. I hopped out at a major intersection, and gave the driver a wave. He gave me a nod. There was

no shot gun on this pick-up truck. I don't think that pick-up trucks with shotguns

are too keen on picking up cannery workers anyway.

My route, to the extent that I had the thing mapped out was to take me across

the border, into the Yukon Territory, briefly, then back into Alaska proper, and

down to the coast, where the blasted ferry would be waiting, if I could make it on

time. There is one actual road that runs all the way from the state of Washington

up to Anchorage. It's called the Alcan and someone had taken out the concession

on making bumper stickers saying

"This car drove the Alcan."

That's how long the route is, and how remote the destination. If you make it, you

get a bumper sticker. But I wasn't going that way. I was going in style, sleeping

on the open deck of a boat as it meandered its way south amidst blue waters and

ice burgs, assuming I could make it to the starting point.

I did get another ride out of Fairbanks, this time in the passenger seat of a

beat up blue Volvo. The car was driven an older man who had "left it all behind,"

and gone to start a new life in the North. By "all" I gathered that he meant, a

family, a house and a steady job. He'd picked up and walked out, and he wasn't

embarrassed to talk about it. He was holding down some kind of maintenance job in an outdoor operation that he didn't specify. But there was something about being up in Alaska that made it all make sense for him. He seemed happy to be able to help me along. Maybe I reminded him of one of his kids, because there was some sorrow involved as well.

"Well, I'll be seeing you," he said, as he slowed the car to let me out.

"Yeah, I'll be seeing you," I said.

I gave the door a push and it clicked closed.

"Take care," he called through the open window,

"Take good care," he repeated.

I waved as the car pulled away from the curb and started slowly down the road, gathering speed as it drove off.

I'd arrived in some non-distinct intersection of two non-distinct roads, somewhere in eastern Alaska. To tell you the truth, I didn't know exactly where I was, but it was quite clear that this day was through. There would be no more hitch-hiking. It was time to get some rest. I found a wooded area, nothing more than a patch of trees, off to one side of the road, and I set up my tent. This was really it. The real hobo's life, laying down for the night where ever chance had landed you, with nothing over your head but a layer of orange canvas. I was a little nervous, but not really discontent. I set things to right, as best as I could, stowed my pack at the foot of my tent, and crawled into my sleeping bag. And I lay there and thought a little.

I reached for my wallet, a maroon canvas affair, and took out Connie's picture. She was still smiling, in her slightly embarrassed kind of way. I looked at the picture for a while. It wasn't a game, really. There were plenty of genuine emotions here. I'd gotten stuck. I may not have been in love, that had only happened once, but my emotions were firmly lodged in one place, in this girl's smile, in this girl's eyes, even in her laugh, which I could almost hear, and in her wry almost sarcastic turn of phrase. There had been no intercourse. That was just not part of it, there had barely been a kiss exchanged, but there had been a connection, a connection only broken some twenty-five years later. I put the picture back in the wallet and placed the wallet carefully in the corner of the tent floor. What difference did it make that it wound up in the corner? None, I guess. But that is where it went. And I lay there.

The road outside was still, very little traffic this time of night. The occasional car drove by, its headlights illuminating the sidewalls of the tent, briefly, as it swung by. There was the sound of the wind in the leaves of the trees, blowing quietly. I thought about one of my housemates back in Ithaca, the guy who'd had a friend who knew about Homer and the beach. He'd told storied about hitch-hiking and laying down by the side of the road for the night. Well, now I'd done it. Some kind of initiation or right of passage, no Bar Mitzvah presents or speeches, just I guy who couldn't get another ride and had to make do as best he could. I was pretty tired. I dropped off to sleep.

I opened my eyes with a start. It was Saturday morning, and the ferry was leaving Haines at ten o'clock Monday, morning. How would I get there? And what would happen if I missed it? The next ferry didn't leave for another week. What about registration? What about class? What about Connie? The situation was more serious than I had acknowledged. I pulled my legs out of the down sleeping bag, and flew into action. It's slightly inappropriate to speak about flying into action, when your next activity is going to be standing by the side of the road with your thumb out. There just isn't a whole lot of action there, unless someone decides to stop, which is almost entirely beyond your control. I had two full days of travel time ahead of me, which could be plenty of time, if I got good rides, or wholly inadequate if I didn't.

There was a small grocery store at the intersection, and I stopped in for a pint of orange juice and a banana. The man behind the counter looked me over, and as he returned my change asked me kind of slow,

"Where are you going?" with an emphasis on the "you."

"Haines," I answered, trying to sound at least somewhat confident.

"Road goes through the Yukon Territory. Ain't nobody interested in taking a hitch-hiker across the border. Way too risky." He turned toward the back of the store and began adjusting the menthol cigarettes on the wall behind him.

"Well here's a new one," I thought as I walked out the door, and picked up my pack which I had left by the front step.

"Now they don't want to take us across the border, what next." I thought to myself.

But there was really nothing to be done. There were no buses, certainly no way to call a car service. There was only one way to travel, by means of your thumb. I set up by the side of the road to continue my journey. But this time I had some company, another hitch-hiker came strolling down the road, evidently having gotten an early start, and been let off a ways back. He was carrying a small black book in his right hand and he gave me a friendly wave.

"'Morning," he called out.

I waved in return.

"How's it going?" he asked as he walked up.

"So far so good," I answered taking him in.

He was a tall skinny guy, in loose fitting blue jean painter pants, and a simple dark blue T-shirt. He wore wire rim glasses and his curly dirty blond hair was tossed and tasseled.

"I'll move further on down the road," he volunteered.

This was common hitch-hiker courtesy, the guy who came last move further away from the on-coming traffic.

"No problem," I said.

"Where are you from," I asked.

"Wisconsin, been traveling for close to a year. Good company," he pointed to his book, and held it up for me to see.

It was a small book of poems.

"I memorize them while I wait," he said.

This struck me as an awfully constructive use of time, but I didn't say anything.

"Well, I'll be seeing you," He waved again and started walking up the road.

"Be seeing you," I said.

It was the first time I'd actually made friends with another hitch-hiker on the road itself, and we crossed paths a couple of more time that day before nightfall when we both arrived at the famous, or infamous town of Tok, Alaska. Tok has the distinction of being the last town, city or metropolis on the Alaska side of the

Yukon boundary, the line that separates the great state of Alaska which is a proud member of the United States of America, from the Yukon Territory which resides firmly in another North American country, namely Canada. It so happens that these two countries get along quite well together, both being relatively prosperous and at peace, but the fact remains that there is an international border here. The border is not policed. There is no barbed wire, or watch towers with dogs or search lights. But however innocuous the side road may appear, the police departments on their side do have every right to stop and search cars passing from one side to the other.

Drivers in these parts are aware of this fact. They are also aware that while many hitch-hikers may be fine upstanding citizens, others may be prone to carry small amounts of marijuana or any one of a number of other illegal substances. They are also aware that if these substances are found in their automobile, they are liable to held responsible. For all these reasons, Tok, Alaska, has become infamous as the hitch-hikers great pit, holding pen and waiting area. The place where many are let off, and few depart, at least not without a prolonged period of waiting. And a prolonged period of waiting was exactly what I didn't have. I was stuck in Tok, Alaska. Sounds like the title to a folk-rock song, which I never wrote. Kind of like being stuck in "Lodi Again," I guess.

I arrived in Tok somewhere around four or five in the afternoon, and that is just where I stayed for going on a day and a half. I toughed it out for a few more hours that first night, but got nothing. I was still optimistic. I had until eleven o'clock Monday morning, and it was still only Saturday. A couple of good rides and I'd be in Flynn, reclining on the deck of that ferry and taking in the sights. I bedded down for the night. Being an old hand by now at this roadside sleeping, it didn't faze me a bit. That might be overstating the matter, but I passed the night somehow. The next morning, I realized that I wasn't the only hitch-hiker stranded in Tok. I emerged from my tent to see a tall blond man passing by. We caught each other's eye, and I said hello,

"Good morning," I said, not fully awake.

"I'd like to stop, but I have to go for a beer," was his friendly greeting.

He was German, as was clear from his accent, and possibly partially by his choice of breakfast beverage.

He and a friend were camped out in a small woods just up the road. I spoke of Tok, as a metropolis. That was entirely facetious. The town of Tok, was really nothing more than an intersection with a gas station. No general store, no post office, certainly no town center or suburbs. Tok existed on the map, but on the road, you could pass through while changing the radio station and never realize you'd missed anything. At the moment it was a place I wanted to get out of as quickly as possible, but once again the speed of my exit was controlled by forces outside of myself. I struck my modest roadside camp and positioned myself by the side of the road. But nothing happened.

There wasn't a lot of traffic to begin with, but no one stopped. The locals didn't even slow down. They saw another cannery worker headed south and they drove by without turning their heads. There were tourists as well, RV's, mobile homes, but somehow the word must have gotten out. You don't really want to have a stranger in your back seat when passing through an international border. They all drove by. And so the day proceeded, hour after hour. I got creative, boredom can do that that. I'd do a dance, wave, flash a sign around, I'd made a sign. But nothing seemed to work. I seemed to be stuck in Tok. There was a small triangular patch of grass at the intersection and I tried to strike up a conversation with a couple of French tourists. You'd think all those years of repeating what I'd had for my petite dejeuner in French class would be good for something, but, once again, no luck. The afternoon passed into evening.

This was indeed becoming serious. I had no back-up plan, other than to spend a whole week in the town of Haines, waiting for the next ferry, and I had not even begun to calculate how badly that would throw off my plans from there on out. Evening came on, then night. I didn't even think about going to sleep. I

had one more night to get to Haines, the ferry was pulling out at eleven o'clock the

next morning, and if I missed it there would be plenty of time to catch up on my

rest. There was only one other option, the gas station, which remained open all

night. The light was on in the small front room, and I pushed the door open.

Inside, beneath a three-bulb neon light hanging from the ceiling was an

Indian man sitting behind a low counter. He had his young son with him. The kid

was sitting on the floor pushing around a red toy fire truck. They both looked up

when I came in. It was pretty clear I was not looking for gas. The kid had large

brown eyes and jet black hair. It seemed a little strange to see such black hair on

someone so young, but that's the way it was. The office was not in any terrific

state of order. Things seem to have been left pretty much way they fell, oil

treatments, gas filters, some spark plugs, a few jumper cables. They were all there,

some hanging on walls, others left on top of filing cabinets. The guy sold gas. All

this other stuff was secondary. I gave the pair my best friendly greeting. This was

the only show in town, the only all night establishment in Tok, the only place with

a light on where it might be possible to establish human contact with someone

driving east.

What the two thought of me is anybody's guess, but they didn't get too worked up about seeing me come through the door. I stood around and exchanged

pleasantries with the man. We didn't talk all that much but the little guy was

interested in my guitar case, so I took out the instrument seated myself on the floor

with my back to the wall, just to the right of the filing cabinet with the jumper

cables on top, and played. They both listened. The kid forgot about his fire truck.

This was more interesting. And it struck me, as I sat there strumming my guitar,

that I was a long, long way from home, from the library stacks, from Ithaca and all

that I had sought to leave behind, sitting on the floor of a gas station in the small

hours of the night, somewhere in eastern Alaska, strumming a guitar. I know this

is not an original thought. I'd been there before. But this time it really hit home.

Every so often, a car or a truck would pull in for gas. Sometimes the car was

heading west which did me no good at all. Sometimes they were heading east, but

had no interest in taking someone else along. I kept at it. Then it happened. A

dark blue pickup swerved into the lane in front of the gas pumps and came to a

rest. It had a cab on the back of the truck bed, an enclosed fiberglass roof, fitted

over the sides of the truck with a hatch back opening in the rear. I had a good

feeling. The Indian man went out to pump the gas. The kid was half a asleep in a

wooden arm chair, his fire truck still in his hands. I strolled outside trying not to

look too concerned. The driver had a partner. The two were standing to the right of the truck looking up at the night sky and talking quietly. I walked over.

"How far are you going?" I said, not wanting to seem to be interrupting their conversation.

They stopped talking and looked at me. They looked at me pretty good. It was close to mid-night in a darkened gas station. I tried to look friendly. I smiled. I shifted my weight from one foot to the other. They kept looking.

"Who really wants to know?" The driver asked me.

So I started in. I explained the whole thing. Haines, the ferry, being stuck in Tok, the week lay over, I may even have thrown in something about a college registration. And when I'd finished, the driver said.

"Climb in back."

"Wow! Thank you!" I said.

They continued their conversation as I scampered inside the gas station office to pick up my pack and guitar. The little guy was out cold but I said good-bye to the Indian man and walked outside to continue my journey.

I stowed the orange Kelty on one side of the truck bed and slipped my guitar in behind it. I opened the hatch-back wide and climbed in. The gas had been paid for and we were on our way, off into the Alaskan night. They knew just where I was going, but there was still one small hitch. They would be letting me off at

Haines Junction, not Haines itself. From my passing knowledge of the Alaskan road map I knew that Haines Junction was about two hour's drive north of the port itself. I'd still need one more ride. But I set those thoughts aside. I was moving, forward, and that was a relief. I lay back and took in the view through the dirty glass window on the back of the truck's hatch back. I started to get a little sleepy. The road was dark with only the occasional car coming from the other direction and passing out of sight behind us, its rear lights lost among the still green trees of late summer, darkened by the night. My eyes closed. I slept.

Through my broken dreams I felt the hard corrugated metal floor of the truck bed. I heard the sound of the truck engine, shifting gears, accelerating and slowing around turns. On through the night we drove. I also thought I had a chance of making that darn ferry after all. If all went well, we would arrive in Haines Junction in the early morning and I would need only one more ride to make it down to the port in Haines by eleven. Success and a week of on-board relaxation appeared within reach. Sometime around three or four in the morning, there was a rain shower. I heard the rain pattering down on the roof of the fiberglass cab, and saw the splattered mud kicked up from the roadway onto the rear glass panel, illuminated by the retreating lights of the cars moving in the opposite direction. We crossed the border while I was out.

All things taken together, it wasn't such a bad trip. There was certainly some stress here, but there was also a sustained sense of adventure. The rain passed and the new day dawned. The sky grew brighter. There was no way to speak with the two men in the front seat but I could see them through the partition dividing the bed of the truck from the front seat. The truck pulled to a halt at a crossroads.

"Here we go," I thought to myself, as I prepared to remove myself from my cramped metal and fiberglass cocoon. I crawled out of the cab, hoisted my pack and guitar onto the ground and walked up front to say thanks. They wished me well. We'd been in the same vehicle for a good six hours but left knowing no more about each other then we had when we got in. How many relationships can remain that simple? The truck drove off.

Haines Junction, stood somewhere on the population charts just below Tok. If anybody actually lived there they didn't count civic pride high on their list of accomplishments. Like Tok, Haines Junction was little more then a cross roads, with two or three industrial looking buildings on nondescript utility. One road came in from the west and continued, on the horizontal, toward the east, another branched off to the right going south. That is the one I needed to take and I had precious little time to spare. I stepped out of the truck bed at seven am. That meant I had two hours to pick up a ride and two hours to make the trip. There just wasn't a whole lot of leeway. If it took me more than two hours to get picked up, I wasn't going to make it.

This might be a good time to reinforce the idea that this is absolutely the wrong way to employ this means of transportation. Hitch-hiking is the way a man of leisure gets around, the man who has a destination but no time table, the man as interested in the next ride and its driver, as he is in getting where he is actually going. The hitch hiker sets out in the morning with a rough destination in mind, and hopes to arrive some time before sundown, or at least before the end of the week. My attempt to travel from Haines Junction to Haines violated all of these proscriptions. I was in a big hurry and hurry and hitch hiking don't belong in the same sentence, and, I hate to break the news, the passing cars did not choose to accommodate me.

I stood there. I danced. I stood in the middle of the street and danced. I waved a sign around. Nothing, nobody stopped. They really didn't care about my ferry or my ferry schedule. They may have wondered a little at the frantic guy by the side of road, but nobody slowed, nobody pulled over, nobody stopped. The hands on my watch moved relentlessly forward, and by ten o'clock it had become painfully obvious that the ferry would be leaving without me. Even if someone did stop they weren't going to make the two-hour trip in sixty minutes. The game was over. I folded up my sign and walked over to a grassy spot by the woods to contemplate my future.

Certain facts were indisputable. Fall term registration would begin with or without me. I'd made this whole darn trip so that I could pull into town and visit Connie on the way back. Right then, I didn't know exactly how I was going to participate in either of those events. I found a pay phone, yes, there was a pay phone in Haines Junction and called home. I guess I just needed to talk it through with someone. My parents were home and they took the call. There wasn't much they could do, but they heard me go through my options, which weren't terrific. I also tried to reach Connie, it being a suitably dramatic moment, but got no one. I sat on my pack and strummed my guitar. I may have said it before, but a beat-up acoustic guitar is a good traveling companion.

And then it happened. It may have happened before, but this time it really happened. I light blue pick-up truck swerved around the bend and came to a screeching halt just a few feet before me, and seated in the front seat was the poetry man, the guy who knew how to use his time on the road constructively, and a stunningly pretty girl with long dirty blond hair at the wheel. Where they had come from, I couldn't say, but there they were. Poetry man got out and gave me a friendly hello.

"No luck?" he said.

"And then some…" I answered.

We didn't actually shake hands, but it was as though we had.

The girl got out and walked around the front of the struck. Who made

people like this? These beautiful creatures who smile and ride around in the front

of light blue pick-up trucks, I was grateful. She'd picked up one of us, she was

ready to pick up another, and if there had been three or four more she would have

picked them up too. My big problem was that I now didn't really know exactly

where I was going.

I discussed the matters with my new found traveling companions. The

woman, whose name was Carrie, Carrie Smyth, had an idea.

"We're headed through Whitehorse. Why don't you catch a plane?"

Here was an alternative plan. If you can't travel by water, why not travel by

air. It certainly beat stewing in the port of Haines for a week. I jumped at the

offer.

"When do we leave?" I said.

And just like that we were off, headed back into the Yukon Territory that I

had passed briefly through the night before. Except now it was daylight. The sun was shining. No sign of rain, just three friends riding in the front of a light blue pick-up.

They brought me right to the airport, helped me find a flight and waved to me as I walked up the stairway leading to the plane entrance. And I never saw or heard from either of them ever again. Maybe it would be different now, in the age of e-mail and Facebook. But would it really be any better? They stood side by side, Carrie and poetry man, behind a wire link fence on one side of the tarmac, and the plane taxied away. Was their friendship any less real or valuable because it was so short lived? Does reconnecting with someone you once knew, twenty-five years later, make them any more of a friend, or does it just expose the fallacy of trying to perpetuate an image created in one era in another?

Hitch-hiking may be an unusual way to get around, but air travel is, in fact, far stranger. One minute you step through a small, oval, metal door in one city, and an hour and half you step back through the same oval, metal door in an entirely different city. Talk about disconcerting. It has no flow, no rhythm, no continuity. Yes, you can look out the window and get some sense of where you are going, if you are not above the clouds, but the whole thing is just not organic. You generally arrive and leave on time, but the passage through space is distorted. My plane touched down on Vancouver Island. It was a short trip. I ate the salted almonds. Who decided that airplanes should serve salted almonds? Probably the salted almond salesman.

Vancouver Island, as distinguished from the city of Vancouver itself which lies on the mainland in the province of Vancouver, talk about confusing, is very British. I didn't have a whole lot of time to walk around but I saw some kind of capital building which was grand and Victorian and firmly of the empire, surrounded by a very British looking garden. From there it was another ferry ride which took me back onto American soil, into the city of Seattle, in the later part of the evening. I had someone to look up in Seattle, a high school classmate who had flirted with the idea of coming up to Alaska with me. Instead, he'd spent the summer as a student at the University of Washington, learning Russian, certainly a more productive use of his time, but probably not as much fun.

He was waiting up for me in one of the student lounges and we hung out for a while. Over the next few days he showed me around the city and we took a trip to one of the smaller islands in the Peugeot Sound and I lost my tent. That's right, it fell off the back of my pack as we were scampering through some underbrush and I never saw it again either. But things were drawing toward a resolution, and I wouldn't really be needing that tent any more anyway. When we parted, Les, that was his name, Les, gave me a stone with a circle of white quartz running around the circumference, intended to symbolize a never ending friendship. It was a fine and noble sentiment.

I got on a bus, a Greyhound, and headed down the coast. This was supposed to be one of the highlights of the trip back, watching the Pacific Coast as the bus traveled along route 101. I'd looked at pictures of it a million times. I'd grown particularly fond of the view from Route One in northern California, as featured in the opening credits to a film starring Chevy Chase and Goldie Hawn, whose name escapes me. Barry Manilow is singing about being ready to take a chance again as this small car negotiates its way down a curving road above the rocks and spray. I thought that was just great. For that part of the trip my bus was inland but I did get a pretty good view of the rocky spires jutting out of the water along the Oregon coast line. After we veered left at the town of Fort Bragg, we traveled in land, not failing to lay over in the Red Wood National Forrest. I bought a wooden box as a gift for my sister and marveled at the height and majesty of those trees.

But I had a destination in mind. The next time I stepped off that bus, I would be in the city of San Francisco, by the bay, as some song goes, and that would be something. We arrived at night, and I immediately called Connie. I'm quite sure Odysseus did not have phone service when he arrived home, with which to call Penelope or son Telemachus, but I wasn't taking any chances. She answered the phone,

"Hello," her voice sounded small and far away, especially considering that she was just across town.

I was tempted to say, "Je suis arrivee," but I refrained.

"I'm at the bus station," I said instead.

"Come on. Come on over." She was moved, but her voice also had some of her trademark sarcasm.

And that's just what I did. I rode the subway. I walked up a long hill, and I entered a cooperative home on the out skirts of Berkeley. Connie heard the door close.

"I'm up here," she called out.

She was indeed up there. She was perched high on the sloping roof of the house looking over the Berkeley hillside. I climbed out through a third story window to join her. Did she recognize me right away? There is a passage in the Odyssey where Odysseus and Penelope see each other for the first time and Penelope looks on him "full of wonderment," he is so changed in appearance. Seriously, folks, I'd only been gone for two months. I hadn't fought in any wars or confronted any mystical creatures. All I'd done is freeze some fish and walk around in the mountains. Still the moment had its poetry. We sat up there and talked quietly. It was nice to see her. The next day she took me out for a bike ride.

We borrowed a bike from another girl who lived in the same house and rode clear

across the Golden Gate Bridge and took a boat ride back from Sausalito. I sat on

the dock of the bay and "watched the tide roll away." We had a great day. And

the next day I pulled out. Connie was having some health problems that she didn't

go into in detail about and they had to be attended to. Her brother was there to

help her. So I got on a plane.

And just like that, through the magic of air transportation, I was winging it,

at hundreds of miles an hour over country that would have taken weeks to traverse

by means of my thumb, with or without a sign.

I stopped over briefly in the city and headed back to school, school in the

same town I'd been so anxious to get away from the preceding June. Things

looked pretty much the same. The green on the leaves was a few degrees paler,

but the flow of students to and fro across the campus remained constant. It was

still warm enough to swim in the gorge, and fraternity parties were just getting

underway for the fall semester. Classes had not yet begun. Cornell without the

classes is a remarkable beast. I wandered about seeing the occasional familiar face,

not yet venturing to visit the house many of my housemates had taken for the new

year, but which I had graciously declined an invitation to join. What does the soldier do, newly returned from the war? How does he acclimate himself to familiar streets and scenes from a past life? He walks about. He is there, yet he is not.

The rock band, The Eagles, had a hit in the late '70's by the name *Desperado*. They go on about this outlaw who comes to recognize that his prison, "is walking through this world all alone."

"Freedom, oh freedom, that's just people talking. Your prison is walking through this world all alone."

I still spent more than my share of time walking around the Cornell campus alone. Connie came back, but we didn't see each other all that much that year. I was still a regular at dinner with my old housemates, and cooked once a week, but it really wasn't my house. I returned to my old study habits, in part fueled by a desire for a place on the ever-elusive Dean's List. I stayed up late and still closed the library. In hind sight, I think I have come to recognize that in the words of Al-Anon, "We cannot drop out of human involvement without endangering our spiritual health." Every effort to reach out toward others during those college years brought its own reward. My own passivity may have invited trouble, but I established connections, connections to the world around me, which are in fact invaluable.

Then there is the question of Don Quixote and madness. The knight errant concludes his tale with these words,

"I was mad; I am now sane; I was Don Quixote de la Mancha;

I am now, as formerly, styled Alanzo Quixonao the Good, and

may my repentance and sincerity restore me to the esteem you once had for

me!"

I don't believe my journey to Alaska was madness, neither was my infatuation with the beautiful Connie. Let's just call it youth instead. Unfortunately, that summer also marked the beginning of a long bout with severe obsessive compulsive disorder. My rages became more frequent and my periods of obsessive rumination ever longer. I was becoming very, very sick. Fortunately, my story has had a happy ending. I got the help I needed and I recovered, by the Grace of God, for today. But what about everyone else, housemates, fellow students, co-workers, who only went half way down, who never hit bottom and wound up on the sofa of some psychiatrist's waiting room. Isn't it possible that they are sick too, in their own way, and don't they all deserve the compassion I would grant a sick man?

Now there's a serious way to end a light hearted tale. I went forward, I froze fish, and I came back. You could call the tale "there and back," but I think

Tolkien has already used that line. It was one summer, a summer worth remembering, not dwelling on and rehashing, but setting down and placing on the shelf where it belongs. God speed, and happy trails.

CPSIA information can be obtained
at www.ICGtesting.com
Printed in the USA
BVOW08s2202141116
467855BV00001B/6/P